SAVE Me, KURT COBAIN

Save Me, Kurt Cobain

Jenny Manzer

DELACORTE PRESS

Copyright © 2016 by Jenny Manzer

All rights reserved. Published in the United States by Delacorte Press, an imprint of Random House Children's Books, a division of Penguin Random House LLC, New York.

Delacorte Press is a registered trademark and the colophon is a trademark of Penguin Random House LLC.

Grateful acknowledgment is made to John K. Samson for permission to reprint lines from "The Reasons." Copyright © 2003 by John K. Samson.

randomhouseteens.com

Educators and librarians, for a variety of teaching tools, visit us at RHTeachersLibrarians.com

Library of Congress Cataloging-in-Publication Data
Manzer, Jenny.
Save me, Kurt Cobain / Jenny Manzer. — First edition.
pages cm
Summary: A chance discovery makes Nico, fifteen, believe that not only is Kurt Cobain, lead singer of the 1990s grunge band Nirvana, still alive, but that he might be her real father.
ISBN 978-0-553-52126-9 (hc) — ISBN 978-0-553-52127-6 (glb) — ISBN 978-0-553-52128-3 (ebook)
[1. Fathers and daughters—Fiction. 2. Single-parent families—Fiction. 3. Friendship—Fiction. 4. Family life—British Columbia—Fiction. 5. Cobain, Kurt, 1967–1994—Fiction. 6. British Columbia—Fiction.] I. Title.
PZ7.1.M3375 Sav 2016
[Fic]—dc23
2014045663

The text of this book is set in 11-point Berling.
Jacket design by M80 Design
Interior design by Trish Parcell

Printed in the United States of America
10 9 8 7 6 5 4 3 2 1
First Edition

FOR MY PARENTS, KATHRYN AND RON —
MY TWO BIGGEST FANS

CHAPTER 1

"ABOUT A GIRL"

The day my mother walked away, the snowdrops had just appeared. I never saw them nudging through the ground. They turned up each February, fully formed, standing there like unexpected guests. I thought the tiny white flowers looked like fairy shower caps, drooping off their thread-thin stalks. I was four. I remember touching a petal with my finger. It felt like a soft lower lip.

My mother had picked three from the backyard of the house we rented in downtown Victoria, which wasn't much: a slab of concrete, two lawn chairs, a composter, and those snowdrops. She turned to me and said, "I'm going away. But I'll be back before these flowers wilt." She pointed to the Mason jar that held the three snowdrops. It sat on our Formica kitchen table, which was scuffed white with a faded print of black clovers.

"Can you remember that, Nicola?" she asked. Her voice was calm, more so than usual. She had ruler-straight bangs, a long, delicate nose. There was a thin gap between her front teeth that I imagined you could slide a dime through. My mother, Annalee, was as beautiful as Rose Red in my book of fairy tales. Her nickname for me was Little Early, which I assumed was because I always woke her up.

"I can remember," I told her. She said my name with a sigh. Ni-co-*lah*.

On *Sesame Street* a girl in a cartoon remembered her shopping list—a loaf of bread, a container of milk, and a stick of butter—all the way to the store. Her mother let her go alone. I decided I could remember one thing: my mother would be back before the flowers wilted.

She hugged me and left me sitting at the kitchen table. I remember feeling her long hair, velvet soft and silky. My father, Verne, must have been at his security job at the mall. That's not important to this memory.

What's important is this: each day I sat at that table gripping my blue cup of milk as my father bumbled around making toast or slicing bananas. I watched the flowers fade and wither, and by day three the stalks were bald and dead, the petals scattered on the table.

From then on, I knew two things: I would never, ever believe anyone, and I would never again be called Nicola.

The year she disappeared was 1996. Kurt Cobain was already dead, supposedly having committed suicide two years earlier. Of course, I didn't realize the significance of that event back then. I couldn't even brush my own teeth yet, let alone mourn for a man I didn't know: the man who stole the world.

It would be easy to assume that "Smells Like Teen Spirit" was the first Nirvana song I ever heard. It wasn't. It was "Dive," from a Sub Pop compilation called *The Grunge Years*. My friend Obe, who could enter thrifting as an Olympic sport, bought a secondhand copy and played it for me. The next Nirvana song I heard was "Sliver," the one where Kurt Cobain sings about a kid having dinner at his grandparents' house who wants Grandma to take him home. I remember having this idea whap me in the face like a tree branch: if we met, Kurt Cobain would understand me. He was slight and blond, like me, and I almost always wanted to flee dinners at my grandma Irene's, which usually involved a slab of roast beef. It was Obe who introduced me to Nirvana, which is yet another reason to be glad that he exists.

Byron Oberlin has been my best friend forever. No one else applied for the job. I've known him since I was four and have always called him Obe. We met when I lent him my socks. Verne had packed a spare pair in my little knapsack and I offered it to Obe when his got soaked on the playground. The socks had shiny pink hearts on them; I suppose my mother bought them. Obe wore them, grudgingly, and returned the socks fresh and clean the next day, and I remember thinking it was nice to have a mom launder them for me. His mother sent me a Strawberry Shortcake sticker, too.

So I became inseparable from Obe, who lived a couple of streets away. Both of us belonged to the school breakfast club, which meant we received free bread with no-name peanut butter and juice because our parents didn't have a lot of money. The fact that I had breakfast at school hurt my dad's pride, I think, but he was probably glad someone else was taking care of something, even just one meal a day.

Back then Obe was content to go along with pursuits such as experimenting with the ancient tomato-red Easy-Bake oven Verne found at a garage sale. We churned out cakes that resembled golden hockey pucks until one day the oven fizzled for good. Those cakes tasted like a burnt, sweet sponge. We also constructed Lego spaceships and launched balloon rockets off my front porch. We rode up and down the city sidewalks on our secondhand bikes, and we mashed together holly berries to make secret poisons. We got by. I had no mother to curl my hair or make me a Halloween costume, but to be fair, most of the mothers in my neighborhood had jobs. The dollar-store costumes were cheap and shiny, made from the same thin material as picnic tablecloths.

At age fourteen, Obe finally accepted that no one was going to christen him with a cool rap nickname. (Obe rhymed with "robe," and that's about it, and no one called him Byron.) For a time, he pretended to like Eminem, but

I caught him singing along with Destiny's Child and Britney Spears. Then Obe and I really got into retro music together, listening to alternative bands from the 1990s. I tried to avoid the gazes of the other girls at school. I never had the money to dress in whatever the trends were, and I didn't want to anyway.

Verne worked days, six-thirty to six-thirty, or nights, the same, so Obe and I logged our hours in class and left the school grounds as soon as the bell rang, running off to his house to eat Triscuits with Velveeta, or to my place for popcorn and strawberry Quik. My rented upper-floor suite, though drafty, was preferred, since my dad got home later than Obe's mom. Sometimes Verne would be gone all night if he worked a late shift, but he often played the daughter card. "Gotta get home to Nico," he'd say to his coworkers, reminding everyone that he was all I had.

The nights he was gone I often stayed awake, listening, my fingernails digging half-moons into my hands. Some nights I allowed myself a memory of my mother. I only had a handful of memories, and some were blurred around the edges. I played them over and over, remembering them slowly, *And then this, and then that,* as if letting a sweet lozenge dissolve under my tongue. Sometimes the memory would cheer me up, but often it would make me sad.

I once heard from a counselor that children can form memories earlier than age four—and even as young as two—but they forget them as they get older. I read more about it online and discovered that babies can't hold on to their memories because of their undeveloped limbic systems, as if their little brains are change purses with holes in the bottom. But toddlers can store their memories, at least until they begin fading around age ten. Reading this set off sparks of panic in my chest, because we are what we remember. So I review my memories. I make sure all the pieces are there, and then I put them away again. I told Obe I would never become a serious boozehound or a junkie, because I can't damage my brain. I don't have much else.

By the time we reached grade nine, afternoons usually involved marathon music-listening sessions at my house. Obe would sit cross-legged on the carpet. He was amazingly flexible, thin and frail, with the posture of raw bacon. He had dramatic glasses: thick black frames and wide, round lenses that would have been distracting had it not been for his hair, which sprang from his head in wild curls that resembled punctuation. He was not adored at school, but he wasn't tormented, either. He was lucky to be a boy, I figured. Boys don't have to be super good-looking. They can compensate with skills.

At school I alternated between sleepwalking and having fits of anxiety when anyone noticed me. Not much worth mentioning happened that school year until October, when I got my first Nirvana album.

"Obe, let's get out the Ouija board," I said, handing him a glass of Coke. (It was actually cola. Verne bought generic everything.)

"Nico, not again. I'm tired of that stuff. I thought we were going to Lyle's Place."

Obe and I loved Lyle's Place, a CD store downtown next to a movie theater. You could buy pricey imports from Britain or get domestic albums cheap and used. The store's logo has a teal cartoon Martian with a half-moon smile. He was riding a spaceship. Obe and I went there all the time to paw through the discs. We never stole anything and usually scrounged enough money to buy a CD every couple of weeks, so our presence was tolerated. I badly wanted an iPod, like other kids at school had, but there was no way I could afford it.

Lyle's Place also sold magnets, T-shirts, and other mass-produced novelties people buy to appear unique. Once Obe bought me a button that read *Jesus loves you, everyone else thinks you're an asshole.* He meant it to cheer me up, but later I hid it in my underwear drawer and cried. Deep down, I feared that everyone at school *did* think I was an asshole except Obe.

"First the board, then Lyle's," I suggested. I liked any excuse to leave our run-down house. Obe sometimes tried to put his foot down, but he wasn't good at it. He was smart, but he didn't like dealing with details, so I made most of the decisions.

While Obe ate popcorn, I whipped out the Ouija board, which had once belonged to my mother. I couldn't stop asking it questions. I didn't need a shrink to figure out that I wanted answers about her. Of course I did.

"Okay, but just three questions," said Obe, gesturing to make his point. He'd taken to wearing fingerless gloves, no doubt inspired by something he'd read. His parents were divorced, barely spoke to each other, and Obe would almost always rather back down than raise his voice. He'd heard too many fights in his lifetime already.

"Will my mother ever come back?"

We put our fingers on the board. I could feel it hum after a few minutes, like the tiny heart of a bird. The pointer trembled, then lurched forward, moving dead center toward the YES and the NO. The pointer quivered toward the NO, then staggered in the direction of YES.

"Nico, I don't think this is good for you," Obe said. The gloves were ridiculous, gray and black.

"Who are you, Dr. Phil? Concentrate. You're bringing bad energy."

"I don't think we should mess with this stuff, Nico. The other side."

"You didn't say that when we were asking all those questions about that girl you were so hot for, Sari . . ."

"Yeah, okay, that was dumb."

The pointer was stuck between YES and NO. I wanted to try another question. A big one. "Is Verne my real father?"

Obe rolled his eyes as the pointer shuddered toward NO. I felt something flip in my stomach.

"When will I meet my real father?"

I waited, examining my fingernails, which looked wretched. I had put black polish on them and then just let it chip off. Obe sighed. The pointer was on the move, heading to the numbers.

"One, four," I said. "Fourteen. I'm fourteen."

"You're almost fifteen."

"Maybe it means fourteen days."

"That's two questions, Nico. Let's go now."

The farther I got from my lonely house, the better I usually felt.

"What are you looking for?" Obe asked me as we walked along Douglas Street, the city's main drag.

"I don't know," I said, shoving my hands in the pockets of my shorts, which I was wearing over leggings. I'd forgotten what was on my album wish list. I could feel sadness welling in me again, a cold pool.

"Well," said Obe, who had a sixth sense for knowing when I needed a boost. "You're a hard, angry young woman, and you need hard, angry music. Nico Cavan, do you know the date?" Obe liked to talk in a theatrical way sometimes, as if he were in an old-time movie, wearing a tux. He also did his research, checking out armloads of music magazines from the library. He always knew what I'd like.

"It's October 5, 2006, and starting to piss rain, Obe." I took my hand from my pocket and linked my arm with his, as we liked to do. I remember it was a Thursday, because it was right before Thanksgiving weekend.

"Oho, yes. And it's the day you're going to get your own Nirvana album. *Bleach*, to be precise."

"Just as long as I don't have to drink it," I said, trying to sound bored, but I felt a shiver like icy fingers on my rib cage, like something was about to happen.

When I was small, Verne was afraid I'd plop off a slide and break a bone and he'd never know because I wouldn't cry when I was injured. I'd just keep walking. I have a high tolerance for physical pain. What I can't stand is minor annoyances: a thread of celery between my teeth, a scratchy clothes tag. Those drive me insane.

Verne was a security guard at the university, often working nights patrolling residences and chasing drunken rich kids out of parking lots. He mostly caught eighteen-year-olds doing stupid shit involving too many vodka coolers. He broke up the fights, got students to put their clothes back on, go back to their dorms and sober up, or called the city police if need be. One year he found that some first-years had been growing marijuana in Finnerty Gardens, an area of native plant beds near the Fine Arts building. That was a professional highlight for him.

He had a live-and-let-live attitude with me, though. "Nico is who she is," I heard him tell Grandma Irene, who had just moved to an old-age home in Oak Bay, a swanky suburb near the ocean. Then a deep sigh. Verne, as I thought of him, was a solid appliance of a man—wide-chested and long in the body, with olive skin. My mother, I know, was the opposite: reed-thin and pale.

My mother never did come home. Nor was she found, living or dead. She became, at age twenty-eight, a missing person. I can remember being five and watching my dad get ready for work, putting on his uniform, and I couldn't believe how he could carry on driving, and dressing, and frying food, and watching the Canucks play hockey. There was a police file, sure, but lots of women in Victoria walked away from their lives and never came back. There were leads from time to time, phantom sightings, an idea that she had gone to New York or even Ireland, as she had always joked of doing. She loved old songs as well as harder, alternative music. None of the theories brought her back. I always told myself to expect the worst. Once, when I was ten, my dad and I were sitting at Willows Beach drinking hot chocolate from Styrofoam cups. We were quiet, watching dogs fight each other on the sand, the waves crashing. Off in the distance I could see a cluster of sailboats.

"How could she leave somewhere so beautiful?" I asked Verne. I don't know why I said that, because she didn't leave the ocean, she left our moldy rental house with the kitchen cupboards that didn't close properly. She left *me*.

Realizing that Verne would never broach certain subjects, I tried to stay one step ahead of the game. I learned about girl stuff from paperback books. Verne didn't like to talk. He liked to play road hockey (I indulged him sometimes) and watch movies (this I actually enjoyed, too). Our finest evenings spent together began with spaghetti and garlic bread, followed by a movie, using one of North America's last remaining VHS players. ("Hey, it still works" would be Verne's catchphrase on a sitcom.)

Verne rarely went out when he had time off. He probably couldn't afford a babysitter, or maybe he had nowhere special to go. We generally stayed home at night. The house was in a sketchy part of downtown that was neither hip nor cosmopolitan, next to a business that laundered service uniforms and shipped them off in green vans. Most people in the neighborhood were decent, but one morning in the playground, Obe and I found broken glass planted right at the bottom of the slide. That sucked.

Verne loves movies, whether they rate two stars or five. So instead of going out, we watched and rewatched masterpieces like *Mrs. Doubtfire*, *E.T.*, and *Lady and the Tramp*. He had no problem indulging my cinematic whims. He would sit peacefully and watch *Desperately Seeking Susan* or *The Breakfast Club* as long as I didn't keep asking him "Tell me how you met. What was she wearing the last time you saw her?" All I knew was that they had met at Mayfair Mall. My mother was a part-time environmental studies student at the university. She also worked in the mall at a candy store called Sweet Dreams. Verne used to stop and make small talk on his breaks until he worked up the nerve to ask her out. That's about all I got out of him.

"I can't talk about it anymore, Nico," he'd say. "Please, don't ask me."

Verne wouldn't give me answers, but he was diligent in providing what he could. By the time I was in middle school, his wages had increased enough that I never lacked for pencil cases and protractors or new jeans in September. He even made my school lunches until I declared myself a vegetarian and begged that he cease and desist with the ham and cheese, ham and cheese, ham and cheese.

Inspired by my new Nirvana album, I decided to go grunge by hacking my best jeans into cutoffs and wearing them with long johns and a Salvation Army plaid shirt.

I previewed my new look at Thanksgiving, which was just the two of us, since Grandma Irene was off visiting her sister. I knew the dinner would be pumpkin pie from the bakery, a turkey breast for Verne, and soy sausage for me, because meat is murder. We still had the same white kitchen table from when my mother left. I'll bet four out of five therapists would recommend that my dad trade it in.

"Isn't that a guy's shirt?" he asked, nodding to the blue-gray flannel.

"It might be. It's the fashion these days," I lied.

I stabbed at the veggie sausage he had cooked for me. It reminded me of a pet's chew toy, fake and rubbery, but I didn't care as long as it wasn't real meat. I had been nagging Verne to cut out the meat. He had some kind of cholesterol problem that he refused to discuss.

"This is good, Verne," I told him. I'd recently started calling him Verne instead of Dad; it was a thing. He hadn't pressed me about it.

Verne had made steamed broccoli and brown basmati rice, too. The rice was still crunchy in places, but Verne did his best. I was no cook, either. We both looked forward to pizza night.

"Are you excited to go see Aunt Gillian?" He sounded hopeful then, his big square face widening, preparing to smile. He worried that there was no one around to teach me how to be a girl.

"Yeah, I'm stoked," I said. Verne and I usually went together twice a year to visit his sister in Seattle. As a fifteenth birthday present, I was going to be allowed to take the Clipper ferry over on my own, with my aunt meeting me on the other side. The trip was booked for the beginning of the Christmas holidays just after school ended. I would return for Christmas Eve.

Whenever we visited, Gillian kept me overscheduled and overcaffeinated. Despite being siblings, Verne and Gillian weren't much alike. Gillian was a nurse, a redhead, a doer, and a talker. My dad was hesitant and quiet. He kept to himself. They say the test of an introvert is whether you find it energizing or draining to socialize with big groups of people. Dad and I both found it difficult, one of the things we had in common. After a day out in the universe, Verne and I would collapse on the faux-leather couch and watch a movie together, grateful not to talk. Me: with my flat, wheat-colored hair and tiny hands. He: with his paws like dinner plates, his thinning curly red hair. We looked nothing alike. The one thing I had of my mother's was a slight gap between my teeth. Aunt Gillian told me that one day it would be the height of charm, as it was on my mother. My mother's eyes were a soft velvety brown, like bulrushes. Mine are blue and bright, almost garish, like the center of a ring from a gumball machine.

The idea of my mother was a pebble against my heel. Every step forward dug the pebble deeper. I would torture myself, racking my brain for any memories of her. Winter was the worst season, with Christmas, of course, and then February marking her disappearance. When December hit, I would think of her almost nonstop. She talked softly but liked loud music. She wore almond-scented hand cream that came in a white bottle with pink letters. She had a fondness for owls, and collected mugs, candles, cookie jars, and stuffed animals featuring them. But that's not a memory; Aunt Gillian told me that.

Sometimes, though, I still searched thrift stores looking for owl designs, picking up pendants or batik wall hangings with the money I made babysitting a kindergartner up the street. I stored the owl tea towels and other items in a flat box under my bed. Then I bought another box and I filled that, too. If I met my mother again, I would be ready. I wondered why people made so many things with owls. In the west we make owls cute, putting glasses on them in cartoons, but in other cultures they're a bad omen. Associated with sorcery and death. They're scary and beautiful at the same time.

I used to have this dream in which I got to ask my mother questions: Why did you leave? Where did you go? My dreams could be so thick, so sticky, they were like a spiderweb that covered me and pulled me in and under, and sometimes I didn't want to let them go. I was given Tylenol 3s once, when I was seven, after my tonsils were taken out. The pills made me feel as if I had fallen through an ice-fishing hole and was looking up at the world from a deep, numbing cold. They slowed everything down: all feeling, all memory, all sensation. There was danger in that feeling.

Once I had my copy of *Bleach*, I listened to the song

"About a Girl" over and over. It turns out Kurt Cobain wrote it for a girlfriend named Tracy Marander. She helped pay his bills while he was trying to make records but got annoyed with him because he never cleaned the apartment they shared in Olympia, Washington. The two kept turtles and rabbits, because he loved animals, if not always people.

CHAPTER 2

"LITHIUM"

I used to shuffle down the school halls with a little half smile on my face just to show everyone that I was okay, everything was good. Then, in the gym locker room, I overheard a girl say that I must be a pothead or something, with that constant silly grin. So I geared down to neutral. When my fifteenth birthday dawned on December 4, nobody at Victoria High School took notice. I didn't see Obe all day, and no one offered to buy me a carton of chocolate milk or share a celebratory toke. After school, Obe and I walked home, not saying much, an icy rain sputtering. I pulled my hood over my head. When we reached my doorstep, Obe held out a square package wrapped in a copy of the free alternative newspaper.

I glanced at the package, then back at Obe. Kids at school thought he was gay, but I knew he had crushes on girls. Verne also seemed to suspect Obe was gay and hence didn't mind if we spent hours on end together. Plus, it was hard not to like Obe once you got to know him.

Obe was wearing a wool cap that suited him, a small stud in his ear, gaucho-style gray pants that looked like something a Depression-era milkman would wear, and a Mr. Rogers cardigan from his team of stylists at the Salvation Army.

"Hey, Obe, thanks," I said. He had made the card himself. He was no artist, but he did enjoy drafting a rude cartoon. It was of two beavers hanging out in a dam wearing coveralls and ball caps, as if they were mechanics. On the wall was a calendar that said *Real beavers*. I unwrapped the newspaper. Inside was a Sonic Youth T-shirt. It was soft and pilled, with tiny dots, as if it had a slight rash. It had a woman like a cutout paper doll on the front and outfits next to her to wear, except they were grunge style, my style. Don't try; don't care.

"Obe, this is vintage."

"Yep. So are you. Fifteen."

"You're fifteen, too."

"I've had six months to become much cooler than you, December baby."

I'd been hearing it all my life. I was often the youngest in my class, always the smallest. Some sociologists have said that it's better for girls to be underdeveloped and start school at a younger age; otherwise they're restless and promiscuous and, uh-oh, get pregnant, as my mother did at twenty-four. Which is really not that young, I guess, compared to fifteen. I've read up on all these things, thanks to my intermittent counseling sessions over the years, all intended to take the pulse of my mental health. I've read articles in *Psychology Today* and on parenting websites, always trying to stay one step ahead of the therapists. So far, I've managed to score "prone to anxiety but doing remarkably well," with the inevitable caveat "all things considered."

"Obe, you're the best," I said, trying to sound like a plucky girl Friday, except my voice quavered.

"I know." He touched my shoulder lightly. The few kids at school who didn't think Obe was gay might have thought something was going on between us. I regularly crushed on boys, but they never liked me back. My latest secret crush was named Bryan. He had regal bone structure and an English accent, because his parents were from Manchester. He called soccer football, which was cool. Best of all, he drew, like I did. I had noticed him doodling. He would smile at me, but I don't think he even knew my name. No one at Vic High noticed me most of the time, and that was almost the best I could hope for.

"When do you leave for Seattle?" Obe asked. He said Seattle in a funny way, as if it ended with "tell."

"December twenty-first, just after school's out. Three nights there, then back home for Christmas Eve."

"Do you want to do homework together?" he asked, dragging the back of his hand over his face. He claimed the acid in rain made him itchy. Doing homework usually meant listening to CDs, or making lists of albums we wanted, or poring through library copies of *NME* magazine. Obe knew I always got sad on my birthday. He said it sometimes seemed as if I blamed Verne for my mom leaving, but I didn't, not really. I just wondered, *What if?* Isn't that what people do? What if I'd been born taller? What if I we'd won the $50,000 grand prize in the grocery store scratch-to-win? What if I'd been good at basketball? Would people have liked me more?

"I'd better not. Verne's making a birthday dinner, I think." I had this secret hope that Verne would buy me a dog. I had been pining for one for years. Verne always said it wasn't fair to the dog. It would be alone during most weekdays. Plus, it was against our lease. Still, I sometimes brought home library copies of *Dogs in Canada* magazine, hoping the photo spreads of the handsome, noble breeds would win him over. It's not so much that I was hopeful; it was more that I was refusing to give up, which is slightly different.

It was impossible to enter our rental quietly. The house was like an eighty-year-old woman with arthritis. The front door stuck and the oak floorboards creaked. The house was dark and largely fashioned of wood—the floors, the railings, and even a ledge around the ceiling that was meant to display china. An old lady lived in the first-floor suite, which she rarely left. It was strange knowing she was down there, listening. Our absentee landlord lived on the mainland in Vancouver and took advantage of Verne's good nature. We had an old fireplace but could never use it because the chimney needed fixing and the landlord never got around to it.

"Nico, that you?" called Verne from the kitchen. He was listening to a traffic report on the radio even though he had driven home already and it didn't matter.

"Yes, Verne, it's me." Who else would it be? We rarely had visitors.

I could see from the hall that vegetable shrapnel was splayed on a cutting board. The fat red pasta pot was out. I knew he wouldn't want me to help with my birthday dinner, so I went to my room and tried on the Sonic Youth T-shirt. It was a bit long but felt soft against my arms. I listened to the Breeders on my headphones. Obe generally humored my retro tastes, sometimes politely pointing out that it was 2006, not 1996. I'd say, "I'm always three steps behind in everything else—why not in music, too?" I didn't want to talk to other kids, besides Obe, about the music I liked. I had to keep something sacred.

My birthday dinner was vegetarian fusilli, romaine-lettuce salad, and a vanilla cake from the Dutch Bakery downtown. Verne had the cake iced with *Nicola*, then scraped off the last two letters. Even after all these years, he still sometimes used my full name.

"What will you do when I'm in Seattle?" I asked him as our forks scraped our plates. The cake was good, spongy and light, with thick Bavarian cream piped in the middle.

"I'll be working, mostly, cruising around the campus. A few kids stay every year."

"That's sad," I said, trying to ignore the fact that my father was one of those lonely drifters, driving around an empty campus. "International students?"

"Yes and no," said Verne, one of his favorite expressions. If we'd been another kind of family, we would have had those students over, shown them a real Canadian Christmas with a glut of gifts and platters of fattening food—but we weren't.

"Nico, you know I'm hopeless at choosing gifts," Verne began, looking up at me, his eyes shining. "But I got you this."

He slid a white envelope across the table, his hand a big pink mitten. Inside was a card that read *For You, Daughter, on Your 15th Birthday* in puffy gold letters. I ran my fingers along them. I always did that, in case one day I went blind. I wanted to shake the envelope but knew it would be rude. Verne and I could be shy around each other that way.

"Look in the envelope, Nico."

There was a square card with a thirty-dollar gift certificate for Lyle's Place. I kept the card in my pocket while we watched movies that night, and the next day I finally bought *Nevermind*, a full fifteen years after its release, and the follow-up, *In Utero*, for good measure. I holed up in my room all weekend listening to them, only surfacing for bathroom breaks and bowls of Life cereal. The music filled all the cracks in my brain, at least for a time. I put every book about Nirvana on hold at the library and stayed up until my eyes felt as if they'd been through an Easy-Bake oven. When Kurt Cobain played his guitar, he looked weightless, like a blond marionette. I can still picture the black-and-white concert photos of him. Rising up, slamming down the chords, and then smashing stuff.

CHAPTER 3

"SMELLS LIKE TEEN SPIRIT"

The Monday after I bought *Nevermind*, I learned a new trick. I was walking the hall between biology and French class, keeping my head down. I looked up and saw a tall, big-shouldered guy, Liam, veering toward me like a barge. He was old enough to drive and his last name was Tuck, I knew, but he was mean, so nobody bugged him about what it rhymed with. There were rumors that he'd slipped "roofies," those knockout pills, to a younger girl at an end-of-summer party. There were worse things than not being invited to anything, I was learning. I saw him notice me, which was not good. He wore a red-and-white-striped soccer shirt, or football, whatever.

"Dogs in Canada," he said, looking at the magazine I had sitting on top of my books. "That makes sense, 'cause you're a real dog."

I could feel my face get hot, processed the sound of his friends laughing, lockers slamming. Then I heard it: the guitars—Nirvana's "crunchy chords," as music writers called them. Then drums pounding down, and a bass that made you feel like your whole head was reverberating. Then I was in French class, and the moment was over. The music in my head had filled the space where I needed to hear anything or say anything. I knew I was on to something better than Tylenol 3s, those prescription painkillers that make all the edges blurry. I had found something to help me forget myself.

After French class, I·shuffled to the girls' bathroom, careful to hide my magazine under my notebook. My army surplus bag tapped me on the hip as I walked, *whup whup whup*. I had written *God is gay* on it, a line Kurt Cobain claimed he used to graffiti around Aberdeen, Washington, the dumpy town where he grew up. On the other side of my pack: *Nirvana*, in black ink. Kurt Cobain toyed around with various band names, including Pen Cap Chew and even Fecal Matter, which I probably would not have scrawled on my bag.

While washing my hands, I did a review of the graffiti. *Lisa Pick eats dick* was gouged into the towel dispenser, perhaps with an X-acto knife. That was old news. I lingered too long at the sinks, which were covered in strands of hair. Anyone who thought females were instinctively clean had never seen the girls' room at Vic High. There was water slopped all over the floor tiles.

"Oh, God. Who let a boy in here?" It was a senior and

two of her friends, their hair all flat-ironed into silky sub-mission. Pants were snug again, I could see. I observed fashion from a safe distance. All three of them were wear-ing the same tight dark-denim jeans and cropped sweaters, as if they'd gotten a three-for-one special. They all had belly piercings. The smell of their body spray hit me then, a combination of cream-soda float and composting flowers.

I looked at their faces to avoid the wink of their navels. I wore a gray-and-red flannel over the Sonic Youth T-shirt, ripped jeans, suede ankle boots from Value Village.

"What I'm wondering is how a lumberjack got boobs," said one of them, orange-red hair, black top. They all snick-ered.

I played the chorus to "Sliver" in my head, bobbing my chin. I felt the panic settle.

"What I'm wondering is which one of you is Lisa Pick?" I said, only a slight quaver in my delivery.

Then I was heading for the door, my boots sliding on the wet floor tiles. I heard distortion, and grinding guitars, and wheezing, which was coming from me. I had never talked back to people, not until then. Nicola was supposed to mean "victory of the people," but in practice I had al-ways been quiet and cautious, more like "runs with earth-worms."

Some days, I thought it would be easier not to exist at all than to have to go to high school with morons like Liam, who I once heard tell a girl "I've got bigger tits than you from lifting weights." But I was waiting for something: art school, a psychology degree, or the affection of some tall, skinny guy who played bass and liked small, blond losers. I had learned to wait, if nothing else, to hibernate, without action or feeling. In animals it had some special name: torpor or something. You power down.

Verne wasn't home when I shoved the door open. I hung my wet slicker on a hook by the front door. My boots were soaked. Verne insisted I needed proper rubber boots. In fact, he had bought me a pair (unisex gray) at Capital Iron, a hardware store downtown, but I refused to wear them, and then my feet grew. There was a note on the kitchen table, which was like our diplomatic pouch. All our important correspondence was left there. *Nico, got called in. Mac and cheese in fridge, just reheat. Love, Dad.*

I grabbed my spiral sketchbook and a pack of pencil crayons with exotic names from the counter. Sarasota Orange. Hollywood Cerise. Even the names held promise. Then I mixed up some milk with strawberry Quik powder in a travel mug. I didn't stir it enough, so the top looked like some strange, volcanic pink planet. Squashing the lid back on, I headed to the hall and pulled the red rope hanging from the ceiling. A rickety metal ladder fell down. I had always been afraid of the attic. We kept Halloween and Christmas decorations there. Most of the decorations came from my grandma Irene, and more boxes arrived after she moved to the retirement home. There were also our suitcases, which we rarely used.

The space was more like a nook with beams and insulation than a real attic. There was one small area with flooring, about the size of a cramped bathroom. That was where

I wanted to set up my studio, or at least an easel. Some-day, I thought, the attic would be filled with my paintings, and I could bring a boy up there (Bryan!) and say, "These are all my works."

Sitting on the wood floor, I felt safe, as if I had been tucked into a pocket, snug. There were sometimes break-ins in our area, and my mind went into overdrive when Verne worked nights. Many times I couldn't sleep at all, waiting to hear his key in the lock. Recently I had heard trilling from the attic, which Verne said came from the pigeons that gathered on our roof since the plastic owl up there got swept away in a windstorm.

I meant to tell myself to concentrate, but instead I thought, *Concrete, Nico, concrete.* I took a slug of Quik, the fake strawberry flavor making my lips pucker. I drew the three girls in the bathroom at school as if they were trapped there, like a statue garden. I made big oval mouths, thin praying-mantis arms, and tiny snail-sized ears. Each figure had a cell phone pressed to one ear. The mouths gaped, but the figures were all turned in different directions, no one listening to the person right beside them.

Bright blue circles around the eyes, lead-pencil slashes for eyebrows, wide in alarm. Their feet were trapped in the concrete, their mantis arms swirling around them like fly-fishing lines. *Lisa Pick's revenge,* I wrote at the bottom, and then the date. The attic smelled of wax, canvas tents, and dried earth, which was probably from Verne's old camping equipment. There were cardboard boxes, three large plas-tic bins with lids, and a proper steamer-style trunk.

I looked at my watch. It was 9:15 p.m. I had dinner to eat and homework to do. *Wurrl, wurrrl, wurrl,* I heard. The pigeons? Or a real owl. I was a city girl; I knew nothing about nature. I climbed down the stairs to eat cold macaroni and cheese straight from the container and allowed myself one memory.

I am sitting in the bath, hearing the roar of water filling the tub, which sounds like thunder to me if I lie back and submerge my head. My mother is kneeling on the tile, swishing the water with her fingers to make bubbles from the blue ribbon of liquid soap. A radio plays, but the music fades in and out like a bee zigging and zagging from a room. My mother's hair is tucked up, in a bun, I guess, and she's wearing a pink bathrobe with a round collar. "Chubby you," *she says, smiling and rubbing my arm with a soapy washcloth, and I laugh.* "Chubby little you."

The countdown for Seattle was on. My rational brain knew the Ouija board was silly, but I still wanted to ask it questions. Would I meet the boy of my dreams in Seattle? I had fantasies about doing something wild there but couldn't decide what that might be. Piercings and tattoos were common at Vic High, which had an alternative vibe. The building is an ancient, drafty behemoth that could be a convent or a prison. By and large, kids at Vic High come from families without a Lexus in the driveway—unlike many of the stuck-ups at Oak Bay or the area's private schools.

The trip would be my first time taking the Clipper ferry

alone. I would also be touring around solo, since Aunt Gillian was working during my visit. My departure date was nearing, so after school that day I'd lured Obe over with the fact that I'd done a sketch of him (true) and had acquired a copy of the Pixies' *Surfer Rosa* (false). Really, I needed someone to help me summon the spirits to move the Ouija board. Obe arrived, dusted with a layer of wet snow. He looked like a powdered doughnut.

"You didn't really get *Surfer Rosa*, did you?"

"No."

"Shit. This is about the Ouija board again, right?"

"Affirmative."

"Nico, can you picture what guys like Liam would do to me if they found out I played with a Ouija board?"

"Yes. Okay, I can. I just pictured it," I said, closing my eyes. I was only ever smart-assed and bubbly with Obe. He made me feel at home in my skin.

"I don't like this stuff, Nico." He was still standing in the hall, the snow disappearing from his shoulders. In some kind of stab at geek chic, he wore black earmuffs.

"One last time, and then I promise, no more Ouija board after I get back from Seattle," I said.

"One last time," he agreed. I went into the kitchen and tossed a bag of popcorn into the microwave, sealing the deal. Obe had a thing for popcorn. It made my stomach hurt, so I usually only had a handful. Everything made my stomach hurt. The pain was as if someone had attached clothespins to my insides: sharp pinches.

Obe and I sat in the living room on a battered Oriental

rug that had been in my grandma Irene's house. The rug still smelled heavily of fake lemon air freshener. I placed the popcorn bowl on the rug and lightly touched the pointer, my legs crossed as if I were sitting at a kindergarten assembly.

"What will this Christmas bring Obe?" I asked, my voice raspy. Shit. I couldn't get a cold right before my Seattle trip.

Obe's eyes widened, as if he were surprised that I had asked a question of the spirit world on his behalf. He had still not taken off the ridiculous earmuffs, but who could blame him? The house was freezing. Cold in Victoria was damp. It clung to you like a layer of fish skin. Sometimes the only way to warm up again was a scalding shower.

The pointer jerked along the letters. *F-A-T.*

"Obe, you're going to get fat," I said, but I was losing my voice, and the joke fell flat.

The planchette glided to *H-E-R.*

"Father," I said. It didn't seem to count until someone said the prediction out loud.

"Shit, Nico," said Obe, who rarely swore. "That's not funny. You were moving it."

"I didn't!"

"Well, my dad's not coming back. That's BS." Obe's cheeks were flushed. His dad had left when he was twenty months old, so it had always been Obe and his mom. His father was in the military and lived in Halifax or something. I felt bad that the board had spelled that word, but maybe it was Obe's subconscious talking.

"Now tell us, what will happen to Nico in Seattle? Obe, it helps to concentrate."

He scowled, his hands resting on the board like two pallid tarantulas. The pointer swung to *F-A-T-H*.

"What the hell," said Obe.

The pointer swooped to *E* and *R*, then stopped, as if exhausted.

"I guess the board is messing with us."

"You have a father," said Obe, glaring. "He's going to come home in an hour and make you dinner."

Obe and I knew exactly how to hurt each other, but we made a point of not doing so. Sure, I had a dad, but he had a mother at home, and she didn't work nights. Nadia was sweet, if a bit clueless, and made world-class vegetarian cabbage rolls. She always called Obe "my big kid," like, "Oh, do you want to speak with my big kid?" She seemed to enjoy the fact that Obe was tall, as if height helped a kid with no dad.

We both sat there, freezing, our fingertips touching the pointer. It began moving again, which freaked me out. *H-U-N*.

"Father the Hun?" Obe asked.

T-E-R.

"Hunter," I said. "Father Hunter. That makes no sense."

The pointer quavered toward GOODBYE.

"It's saying goodbye to us," Obe said, his eyes wide.

"Goodbye," I said out loud. You always had to say goodbye to the board or the spirit might stay longer; that was one of the "rules." The creepiest rule was that if the pointer started counting or doing the alphabet backward, you needed to stop immediately. That meant the spirit was trying to escape and could terrorize you forever. I had never told Obe that part.

"I'm going to turn on the heat," I said, getting up. I noticed that my grandma's rug needed vacuuming. I wasn't big on housekeeping.

"Nico?"

"Yeah?"

"Do you really think your mom used this thing?"

"Dunno," I said, hearing the thermostat click on, a soft snap. "It was hers, apparently. Left in the attic."

"Don't get mad, but I've always wondered, where's all the rest of her stuff? I mean, there's almost nothing here."

"Verne says he waited three years, then gave most of it away to charity. He said it made him too upset to see it every day, her clothes, her books."

"Doesn't that piss you off? That he didn't save those things for you?"

"Yes," I said, and couldn't say more. There was a tangled ball of anger in my stomach. Verne had meant well, I tried to tell myself.

"Do you want to see the sketch I did of you?" I asked, to change the subject. Sketching was the only thing that made my stomach stop roiling.

"Okay. But that's it for the Ouija board," said Obe.

"Yes, I promise," I said, crossing my fingers.

I went into my room to get my sketchbook, considering the answers. Did Ouija boards joke? I had often wondered if Verne was really my father, and once made the mistake of saying that to a school guidance counselor. After that, I'd been forced to attend therapy sessions to discuss my alienation from my dad and whether I blamed him for my mother's disappearance. They even wanted to medicate me. I learned fast to keep my crazy thoughts to myself, or at least restrict them to Obe, who was eccentric in his own, contained way.

"Hey." I tried to sound lighthearted. "Verne will be home soon. Do you want to stay and have dinner with us? I'll make it." He followed me to the kitchen, so I knew his answer.

"Oh, Lord, Nico. Pancakes or spaghetti?" Obe knew my two specialties.

"Pancakes," I said. "We might even have frozen blueberries."

He swung open a cupboard and reached for the top shelf, because he knew exactly where we kept the mixing bowl.

CHAPTER 4

"HEART-SHAPED BOX"

A tsunami of schoolwork crashed down on me, and my brain seized up under the strain. Putting together sentences was the hardest, and I had left all my English assignments until the end. Maybe I was depressed; who knows? But I pushed through the term's final essays and exams by concentrating on Seattle. The trip was everything. Maybe I needed to leave Victoria, or spend a few days not seeing all the green trucks rumbling by delivering their laundered uniforms. Or maybe I needed a break from the armpit-farting Liams of Vic High.

A short essay still loomed. On "a book that means something to me." As soon as I heard that, my mind was wiped clean, as if I'd never read a book. I decided to find my mother's old copy of *Grimm's Fairy Tales*. I had no memory of her reading the stories, but there is a photo of me tucked under a quilt, cuddling up to Annalee, who is fanning the book in front of her face. The photo, a Polaroid, is dated November 1993. My mother loved Polaroid cameras, the kind where the photo spits right out. Back then, for most cameras, you would have had to take the roll of film to a photo lab. And waiting wasn't one of Annalee's strong points.

The book had been passed on to my mother from her own grandparents and was really old, like from 1927, with the title in gold script. The illustrations were by an artist called Rie Cramer. Each scene made you feel as if you were spying on a dream. I used to keep the book in my room, but I hadn't seen it for a while.

It wasn't in the back of the hall closet, wedged in the living room shelves, or under the beds. I stomped around, swearing, and then put my boots on to take my rage out on the storage shed, a place visited by spiders and creatures with long tails. After getting the rusty lock open, I threw boxes and duffel bags of things aside—croquet set, hockey sticks, and sleeping bags. Finally, underneath all that, was a box marked *child books* in Verne's writing. I lifted out *Grimm's Fairy Tales* and closed the box.

My shoulders tensed at the sight of the stack of firewood waiting for the day our landlord fixed the chimney and we could use the fireplace again. A brown spider shimmied down the logs and onto a tied bundle of papers set aside as a fire starter. One of the pages caught my eye: the top strip read *MAXIMUM ROCKNROLL* in black-and-white. The spider ambled away, and I picked up the bundle, slicing the string with a pair of pruning shears. Mixed in with the ancient flyers was a bunch of music zines on different-colored paper, including one called *chickfactor*, a pretty cool name. No way they belonged to Verne. I separated out all the zines and carried them into the house, smoothing them.

I had heard of *MAXIMUM ROCKNROLL*, a punk zine since forever. The faded pink page was turned to an interview with Nirvana, a grainy image of bassist Krist Novoselic (then called Chris, before he embraced his Croatian roots) looming tall in jeans with the knees torn out, and drummer Dave Grohl and Kurt Cobain sitting to his right. Grohl's hair is in a ponytail, and he's wearing a motorcycle jacket. Cobain looks pensive, forearms resting on his knees, his trademark Chuck Taylors on his feet. In the Q & A piece, Kurt is called "Qurt," without explanation. Qurt praises the girl band L7 as being both "heavy and sexy." He and Krist use the word *heavy* more than you'd think was possible.

In the interview, Qurt talks about his knack for writing songs and claims to be writing one for the London Philharmonic, a story about a boy playing video games. He intends it as a metaphor for Nirvana's making it big. The rest of the zine crackles with a crude, exuberant energy, including a "Scene Report" section that includes a "Drunk Punk of the Month" feature. (The winner, shown passed out clutching his guitar, was from a Portland band called Deprived.)

The zine pages had ads from bands I didn't know and a few I did, like Bad Religion and NoMeansNo. I stood in the kitchen, my boots getting mud on the floor, and stared at the zines. There were six in all, and I knew there must have been more. Almost all had one thing in common: an article on Nirvana and their nerve center, Kurt Cobain.

Verne found me at the table, still in my boots, paging through them. He put his lunch box on the counter.

"That doesn't look like homework," he said. "Come on, Nico, you said you have papers due."

"I do. I will. Were these Mom's?" I asked, gesturing to the photocopied pages. Taken at a glance, the zines brought to mind patched-together ransom notes.

"Oh, yeah," he said, trying to sound like it was no big deal, but I saw a ripple of concern cross his face. "Her music newsletters. Where did you find them?"

"They're called zines. In the shed, by the woodpile."

"I didn't know they were there. They look kind of . . ." He gazed at a black-and-white ad for R Radical Records that featured a dog's behind wearing a police officer's hat and sunglasses. "Hey, cop, if I had a face like yours . . . ," it read. It was rude in about six different ways.

"I'll take them to my room," I said, before he thought of confiscating them.

Kurt Cobain would have found the dog ad hilarious.

On the night before the last day of school, I stayed up until 2:30 in the morning finishing an essay on Margaret Atwood's *The Handmaid's Tale*. I woke up at 8:02 a.m. when Verne rapped on my door, causing my Flipper poster (I had sketched the band logo myself) to flop from the wall.

"Nico, wake up. You're going to be late."

I was never late for school. Being late meant drawing attention to myself. I was always on time.

"Shit, Verne, sorry. I was up late with an essay." What had I written? Something about the danger of complacency. Or rather, the danger of accepting a little but giving up a lot. Something like that.

I hefted off my sheets and swung my feet down. It was always awkward for both of us when Verne came into my room, even though there wasn't a girlie thing in sight. Actually, just one: a pink jewelry box that my mother gave me when I was three. Inside was a tiny ballerina that turned around when you opened the box. The ballerina rotated in front of a small, oval mirror with white sparkles making a frame. The box was still filled with a three-year-old's treasures: shiny barrettes, beaded bracelets, gumball-machine rings, and, for some reason, three pink feathers.

"Nico, don't swear," he sighed, and I noticed he looked tired. What he really meant was "Can't you call me Dad?"

I threw on army pants, a gray-green long john–style top. As I ran through the hall past the kitchen, he held out a silver travel mug.

"Coffee, milk, sugar," he said. In his other hand, he produced a small plastic bag that held a bagel from Mount Royal, this place up the street that made real Montreal bagels, or so it was said. I had never been to Montreal.

Still stunned from being yanked awake, I took the bagel and the mug and carried them to the front door.

"Have a good last day of school," Verne said, and then hugged me, careful not to spill the coffee. A little clasp, as if I had a small fire on my pectorals that needed extinguishing. "I might be late, but I'll see you tonight."

I mumbled thanks, yanked my green slicker down from its hook, and started running, not bothering to shut the front door. I remembered that Obe, who usually kept me on track, had an early dentist appointment. The only people I saw as I ran were a guy with a shaved head walking a Mastiff and an East Indian fellow ambling along with his cane. A few elderly people roamed the neighborhood, most in some state of disrepair. Many of the street people used jury-rigged old wheelchairs, and more than once I had ended up pushing one around for a couple of blocks, to help out.

I thought these things as I flew through the streets on my way to school, past the strange urban farm with its big orange school bus covered in graffiti and the fetid stench of manure. I heard the chorus of Nirvana's "Breed" as my feet slammed the pavement. I used to think they were saying "Giselle," like a girl's name, but it was really "she said" repeated.

Perhaps it was fatigue, but when I got to school to hand in my essay with four minutes to spare, I felt tears pricking the corners of my eyes. I unscrewed the lid of the coffee and took a sip. It hadn't spilled. I crammed a hunk of sweet cinnamon bagel into my mouth and walked to the steps of my old, enormous school.

And then I was done. I knew that January would arrive, and classes would start up, but I felt so light on my way home, as if I were stuffed with cotton candy. I would miss sneaking glances at Bryan for a couple of weeks, but my excitement over Seattle trampled that feeling.

I had made it to Christmas break without killing myself, and for grade 9 that was pretty good. Obe had a meeting of his tae kwon do club, so I didn't wait. I jogged partway home, splashing in every cold, deep puddle. My big toe protruded from my shoe like some alien baby; that probably meant I was growing again. I had only one night to wait until Seattle. I needed to pack and to sort my sketches, because Aunt Gillian wanted to see some; she always did. I kind of liked the one I had done of Obe. All my figures had their jaws thrust out and spidery arms like fishing line, as if they couldn't carry any weight. As if they just bobbed along.

The front door was stuck again. When I forced it open with my hip, I remembered that Verne would be late. Sometimes when I was alone, I would turn on all the lights in the house, and the television or the radio, but that evening I went straight to the attic. I pulled down the ladder, and it unfolded like a skeleton. The attic still scared me, but somehow I felt that I could concentrate there.

The attic was lit by only one bald white light, so once up the ladder I switched on my flashlight to inspect the boxes. I spotted my gray backpack right away and tossed it down the stairs. *Whump.* I'd gotten it the year before as a birthday-Christmas combo present for a camping trip we'd planned but canceled because someone at Verne's work got sick and we needed the extra money.

I collected a stack of drawings I had left scattered on the floor and chose four to take along to Aunt Gillian. I was ready to descend back into the real world, down the ladder, when a faded brown cardboard box caught my eye. It had been pushed out from the shadows when I'd been moving around Grandma Irene's boxes looking for our winter hats and mittens. Up close, I saw *Annalee's summer clothes* scrawled in marker. I touched the letters, then pulled my hand back, as if I'd received an electric shock. When I was eleven, I had once used a steak knife to pry out a lamp plug stuck in an outlet. I had wanted to listen to my cassette player. I remembered feeling the electricity enter my hand and run up my arm before I dropped the knife to the floor. The knife was singed black, so I hid it in the backyard. I spent a lot of time making stupid mistakes and then trying to hide them.

My fingers rested on the box. I was touching something my mother had touched. I knew the box couldn't have been there all this time. I had combed the house for traces of her. I had even gone through a *Harriet the Spy*–inspired phase in which I thought that I would unearth the mystery of her disappearance and we would be happily reunited.

Verne had never been a suspect in my mother's disappearance since he had what appeared to be an airtight alibi—he'd been working at the mall. The security cameras had captured not only my father (watching him watching people) but also an altercation at the Toys"R"Us between two customers who wanted the same Game Boy. Instead of focusing on Verne, the authorities' main question seemed to be "What kind of woman would leave a four-year-old alone?" What kind of woman? I didn't know.

I did know: a desperate woman. I had left that part out of the story. She did leave me alone, just for a few minutes, or maybe a few hours. The story goes that she had called a neighbor friend over to babysit. The woman had been late. My mother decided she couldn't wait any longer and left me alone. She had somewhere to be, apparently. I guard that part of the story and try not to think about it, or I'd go crazy and dig up the backyard looking for that steak knife I buried out there when I nearly electrocuted myself.

Sometimes I thought they didn't look hard for her because she'd called that babysitter. It made her seem like a young mother trying to opt out of her life, ditch her kid. I must have told the police she'd said she was coming back, right? I was interviewed, apparently, but I don't remember it. That part has fallen through the change purse. Maybe they wrote her off as a bad mother who didn't want to be found. That was another one of my theories.

My palm lay flat on the box. The cardboard was weathered and soft, like the top of an old person's hand. There was a strip of packing tape lashed across it. The writing was in green marker. Were her clothes inside? Would they smell like her? A sob welled up in my chest like a balloon. I tore the packing tape off. The sound was ragged against the cotton-ball silence of the attic. Why had this been kept from me?

I thrust my hand into the box, like testing the depth of a black lake by diving in headfirst. Instead of the soft cotton of sundresses I felt hard, sharp, plastic. I dragged the box under the light. It was filled with CDs and cassettes. The first one I pulled out was R.E.M.'s *Automatic for the People*. There were dozens of them: more R.E.M., Mudhoney, Sonic Youth, Bikini Kill, 13 Engines, the Lowest of the Low, Dinosaur Jr., Neil Young, and more Neil Young. My mother was more of a music fanatic than I ever could have imagined.

At the very bottom, I found the Nirvana, as if she had packed their albums first. There was a CD of *Nevermind* (the naked baby swimming toward a dollar bill), a cassette of *Bleach*, and a CD of *In Utero*. There was also a cassette of *Incesticide*, a kind of greatest hits album I had not acquired yet but that included my favorite song, "Sliver." I began to cry as I read the album titles, and then I slapped the floor with my hand. Why had no one told me? I banged the floor so hard that pink insulation rained down from the attic ceiling, and even as I cried, I thought that it looked like cherry blossoms crashing to earth.

You see people on the news after some disaster has struck them, a hurricane or a fire, and they're walking around the rubble of their home, picking through the wreckage. They're wearing sweatshirts and jeans. They shuffle. They cry. They hold each other. My world had been overturned, but I was too angry to have anyone hold me. It was as if bees were swarming under my skin. I dragged the box to the top of the ladder, then lowered myself, pulling the box down one step at a time. It made a sound like a peg leg in a ghost story: *thump, shush, thump, shush*. I hoisted the box up, bracing it against my shoulder. I carried it to my room and slid it into the closet, heaping old clothes on top.

The sight of my old Brownie outfit hanging there enraged me. The Brownie pack had met in a church hall, and I had gotten kicked out for going into the boys' bathroom on a dare. There were no boys in the building at the time, but the leader, a humorless woman with eyebrows like hyphens, told Verne I had to go. I was a bad influence, the Brown Owl told him, while Verne stood there in silence. He was still in his security guard uniform, and the irony was probably not lost on anyone. Guess what? The boys' bathroom was nothing great. There were urinals and tidy sinks (because no boys had been there recently) and a towel dispenser, and that was that. The Brown Owl knew I had no mother. She saw my crooked pigtails that looked as if they'd been fashioned by someone wearing boxing gloves.

There is always somebody worse off than you, my aunt

Gillian says. And she should know. In Seattle, she saw all the down-and-out people with no health insurance filling the emergency waiting room with their festering skin infections and dripping noses and cramps from unwanted pregnancies. Verne loved me as best he could. I had a house to live in, my own bedroom, a decent school, and my friend Obe. But I had needed that music.

Kurt Cobain was once asked why Nirvana always smashed their guitars. He said it was a good excuse for not having to do an encore. On *Nevermind* they placed a hidden track after "Something in the Way." It is called "Endless, Nameless," but you have to sit quietly and wait in the silence before it will begin.

I listened to the tapes on my old cassette player and then I listened to the CDs. I played the Breeders' "Last Splash" three times. I had never heard *Harvest* before, so I played "Heart of Gold" over and over until Verne knocked on my door, a polite tap like a saleslady wondering how the swimsuit fit. I lifted my headphones up.

"I'm sleeping. Go away."

I heard him pause at the door. I felt a snarl of pain in my stomach.

"Okay, Nico. Good night." Then a sad mumble: "I love you."

Sure you do, I thought. *That's why you drove my mother away and hid her music from me.* He was a liar, but I couldn't waste time screaming at him. I had a ferry to catch the next day and a backpack to fill. And I had dozens of albums to crowd into my brain.

When I was little, I liked drawing princesses with balloon skirts. I used to lie awake and fantasize about my mother coming home. I still had faith in happy endings. I used to dream that I'd wake up and see her by my bed. She'd be looking over me with such love, such concern. "I'm sorry, Nicola, I never meant to leave you," she'd say.

As I got older, I had nightmares about her. I became aware of people wondering about me—my teachers, my aunt, Obe's mother. How I was doing. By then it seemed certain to them: Annalee would never be found. She was born in Yorkshire, England, to older parents who'd thought they would never have children. They moved to Canada when she was five, first to Alberta, where her father was an engineer, then later to Vancouver, for retirement. Her parents died a few months apart when Annalee was just eighteen. They couldn't bear to live without each other. So there was someone in my family capable of deep, demonstrative feelings, which was a relief. I sometimes wondered how I would be different if I had known my grandparents, if they could have provided the blueprint that I seemed to be missing.

Over the years, I had stopped dreaming of my mother. She became a flicker of a curtain, an idea as unformed as egg white. I'd seen pictures. I'd heard stories. But now I had her music. I might never sleep again.

By morning, I was ready. I had a backpack jammed with my mother's CDs, my CD player, and a wad of flannel shirts, leggings, a second-hand dress, layers of fleece. I slid in my sketchbook. It was only eight-thirty a.m. My ferry to Seattle didn't leave until six p.m. I'd have to avoid Verne for a whole day. I was set to meet Obe to say goodbye. By the time I was back from Seattle, he and his mother would be in Winnipeg visiting Obe's grandparents. Obe went there a couple of times a year. He always came back with strange stories, like how the city has a special night for people to cruise around and show off their cars. I think he liked the feeling of having a full family around him, four people, and who could blame him? It was how things were meant to be—all the booths in restaurants were for four. In some ways two can be the loneliest number.

Sometimes when I started thinking this way I'd feel as if I'd swallowed a burr and couldn't breathe. What if something terrible had happened to my mother? What if she was afraid and alone? Other times, I hoped she'd just hated me and was happy with a new family somewhere. I thought about her every day, of course, perhaps every hour. I couldn't help it. I had seen therapists over the years and was supposed to have coping tools, ways of organizing my thoughts, like a traffic cop trying to prevent collisions and accidents. But since I never caused any trouble, I'd mostly been left alone.

I sat on the carpet, clenching my fists. Then I stood up to make my bed. I would be gone a while.

An hour later, I willed myself to go into the kitchen. My eyes darted to the table, where there was a glass of juice, and I could tell from the deep orange hue that it was the pricey stuff, not from concentrate. French toast sizzled in a pan, the bread making a sighing sound, as if the browning process were painful. I could see three little veggie sausages snuggled up to the french toast. Verne was bent over the frying pan. He wore slouchy gray cargo pants, a turtleneck, a fleece vest. He'd dated a woman a while back, a bank teller, who got him to buy some newer, more youthful clothes. The clothes stuck, but the lady didn't.

"Nico, I made you breakfast—are you hungry?" He looked hopeful. He'd gotten in late the night before, maybe eleven-thirty, which meant he'd been covering a few hours for someone. We always needed the extra money. It was a special breakfast, I could tell. There was a carton of out-of-season strawberries on the counter.

"No, not hungry. Just coffee," I said, to hurt him. I was starving.

"Come on, Nico, we didn't get to have dinner together. I'll fix you up a café au lait, just how you like it."

Verne sugarcoated the fact that I was fifteen and addicted to caffeine with the idea that my coffee was mostly milk.

"I'm going to miss you, Nico," he said, bustling around the tiny kitchen. The linoleum was black-and-white squares that looked like a chessboard. It was cracked, but our landlord never got around to replacing it. The guy just never got his shit together.

"I found the boxes, Verne," I blurted out. "You knew how much I wanted to know about her. Why did you keep her albums from me?"

"Nico, let me explain," he said, putting a mug of coffee on the table. He sighed. Tears filled his eyes. He took a deep breath.

"Your mother," he began. "I, she . . ."

"What?" I wasn't in the mood to be patient. I had waited eleven years.

"She used to listen to those songs, back in the day, those grunge songs. It seemed to always make her sad."

"Make her sad?" Music didn't usually make you sad, did it? Music was like food.

"I don't know," said Verne, shrugging, looking helpless, two shades redder than usual. "I didn't want you to be unhappy, the way she was, listening to that—Nico, I just wanted you to be happy."

"Where were they?"

"At Grandma Irene's house. I put them there until I decided what to do. Then we moved them here when she went to—"

"The home."

"Right, the retirement community."

"I have to go meet Obe now," I said, blinking at the kitchen as if I were in a sandstorm. I could barely walk out of that room, the one I had crawled through as a baby, where I had tried my first solid food.

"Right, Nico," he said. The french toast, dusted with powdered sugar, sat on a plate.

"I'll come back before I leave," I said. And I wanted to leave forever.

⚡

When Obe answered his front door, he nearly dropped the math text he was holding. "Nico, what's wrong?"

I hadn't zipped up my jacket, so I was shivering.

"Your lips are turning purple," he said, pulling me into the hallway so he could shut the door.

"I found a box," I said. "My mother's."

"Oh. Take off your jacket. I'll get you one of my mom's sweaters," he said. I was wearing the Sonic Youth T-shirt.

We sat in Obe's bright yellow kitchen. His mother had sewn a tablecloth with a print of yellow tulips to match. I thought it was cool that his mother could sew. She said she learned to make herself skirts and blouses because she couldn't afford nice clothes otherwise. Nadia had hemmed some pants for me a number of times. I would miss her when I went away.

Obe put the kettle on for hot chocolate. I rambled on. Obe listened.

"Does your mom have any Baileys?" I asked.

"I'm not giving you Baileys, Nico. You're crazy enough right now."

Obe and I strategically pilfered from our respective parents' small supplies of alcohol. We had not yet been caught. I had developed a taste for Baileys Irish Cream. In fact, I sometimes joked about my imaginary friend named Bailey.

"Wow, Nico," he said. "Did you know your mom was that into music? She must have been really awesome." Then he gave me a look, sorry he'd said it. She was the cool mom that I would never know.

"Yeah," I said. "Her record collection was amazing." I was going to say more, but I felt all the energy drain from my body. I had been up all night. I thought about telling Obe that we'd listen to them together when I got back, but I didn't want to share them, not even with him. And I wasn't sure I'd return.

"I'm trying not to hate Verne."

"Don't. Hate him, I mean," said Obe. He'd had experience in hating fathers. "Verne meant well. He wanted to protect you."

"I'm trying," I repeated, but I could feel the hate forming little barnacles inside me. How could Verne do that?

I gave Obe his Christmas present, a Star Wars pillowcase I'd bought online. Obe had always been pissed that his had been stolen at a Scouts' campout. Obe lasted longer in Scouts than I did in Brownies. He was very goal oriented: task attempted, accomplished, reward given. That was the way Obe operated, which was why he aced his courses. I could imagine him writing books one day or being an absent-minded professor with elbow patches.

He thanked me and gave a little laugh of delight, like a

soap bubble popping. He handed me my gift, which was wrapped in a Sears flyer. It was a secondhand paperback copy of a biography of Kurt Cobain, *Heavier Than Heaven*. I'd already read all the books in the library on Cobain, and reread them, including the one that made the case that his wife, Courtney Love, might have had him killed. I hadn't been able to find *Heavier Than Heaven*, which I'd heard was one of the best biographies. The book cover was a black-and-white photo of him, his blond hair falling over his eye, a slight smirk-grin on his face, as if he knows something you don't, but maybe he'll tell you down the road.

"Thanks, Obe," I said.

We had known each other so long that we didn't always have to talk. He had some new CDs, so we listened to them for a while. Obe was on an old ska band kick. After a couple of albums, I got anxious about making my ferry. Verne would be driving me in our small, rusted car that was the color of a dried apricot.

I walked home, feeling hollowed out, swinging the book in my hand. On my way, I stopped at Wellburns and bought a few packets of Kool-Aid—berry blue and lemon-lime—some aluminum foil, and Saran Wrap. When I got home I ignored Verne, went to the bathroom, and got to work mixing the paste. I rummaged under the sink to find petroleum jelly.

"Everything okay?" Verne asked. "Takeoff time in two hours." Verne had been saying "takeoff time" since I was five.

"Yeah," I said, smearing the jelly around my forehead.

The Vaseline had congealed, and was hard, like ice cream. I couldn't remember when we'd last used it. I checked to make sure the bathroom door was locked, then added a big dollop of conditioner to the Kool-Aid paste I had made. I massaged it in my hair, and then shrouded my entire head in plastic wrap, which made it look like a wasp's nest. I had a dollar-store navy knit cap ready to put on.

I pushed open the door, freed from our moss-green bathroom, last renovated circa 1980. My temples throbbed under the plastic wrap. I smelled like sickly sweet fruit punch. When I got to the other side of the water, I would look different. I would *be* different.

CHAPTER 5

"COME AS YOU ARE"

Nirvana's music made me feel better even though it was dark. I had never heard music before that sounded how I felt. Sometimes Nirvana was soft like R.E.M. Other times they were loud, like the Pixies, but mostly they were both at once, soft and loud in the same song. Moody and introspective, then electrified with anger. I was like that, too. I might have seemed soft-spoken, but my thoughts were often raging. When I discovered my mother's hidden albums, I could feel myself turning a corner, as if swinging right into the path of a speeding car. I was silent the whole drive to the Victoria Clipper ferry terminal, which was right downtown on the Inner Harbour, just a few steps from the Royal London Wax Museum. Obe and I used to love that hokey place. We'd always try to hug the figure of Mahatma Gandhi.

"Nico," Verne said as he cranked on the parking brake. December rain ricocheted off the roof of the car. "I know you're mad at me."

"Yes," I said, looking down at my hands in my lap. They seemed pale and oddly shaped, like white coral underwater.

"Don't let that ruin this trip for you. Just enjoy the city and being with Aunt Gillian." The plastic wrap under my hat itched like crazy.

"I won't," I said, still rigid with anger. The car door stuck, so I pushed it hard with my shoulder. I didn't want to miss my ferry. My heart bashed against my chest, because I realized that without my hair showing, I might not be recognizable in my passport photo.

Verne popped the trunk, and I swung my big backpack on, hooking my knapsack onto my shoulder. I tried to march faster than him, but his legs were so much longer that he could easily keep my pace.

"You have that American cash?" he asked.

"Yes." He'd given it to me just before we left.

"Aunt Gillian will meet you at the terminal. Do not go anywhere. Just wait for her. And don't let any strange men sit next to you."

"I won't."

The Clipper terminal was not the most exciting place to start a journey. The chairs and floor tiles were probably about one notch better than the bus terminal, which wasn't saying much. The perky woman behind the counter wore a navy-blue uniform, and her hair was in a tight bun.

"Is this your first time going to Seattle? Traveling alone? Bet your dad's a bit worried. Going to do some shopping, girl stuff, maybe buy some shoes?"

No. Yes. Uh-huh. Maybe. The last one I hedged, not wanting to appear as abnormal as I really was. There was nothing I hated more than shoe shopping, except perhaps bra shopping.

"Maybe you'll go to the Pacific Science Center," the lady suggested. People were always hopeful that I was a normal girl, and I always let them down.

"Sure, that would be great," I said. The smell of conditioner and Kool-Aid hung in the air in a sweet, sticky curtain.

"May I have your passport, dear?" The woman, whose name tag said *Peggy*, wore bright orange lipstick. Coral Snake, I would have called it, if I made up lipstick names. I liked to think about stupid things like that. It made me less jittery. I slid my passport across the table. My hand had made the cover sweaty. She looked at me, and then the passport, and then my knit cap. My passport shows me with puffy blond hair. In the photo, I looked pensive, as if taking an eye exam.

I had arrived at the ferry terminal an hour early, as per the instructions on the ticket. I was sweating under my hat, and worried that a blue drop would roll down my forehead.

"Nicola, here are your documents back. You can take them over there now," she said, gesturing to a guard in a gray uniform. I winced at hearing my full name, then realized that I had made it through step one. "It's

57

passengers only after that point, so best give your kisses and hugs now."

I imagined Peggy to be a scrapbooker, maybe someone who canned her own fruit. That might be nice, having peaches off-season.

"Thank you," I squeaked.

Verne stood, looking tall and conspicuous, as if the phone booth thing from *Dr. Who* had landed in the Clipper terminal. The Tardis.

"Have a great time, Nico. Enjoy your birthday present. When you come back, we'll have our Christmas together, okay?" Verne clamped me in one of his bear hugs then, a squeeze and release.

I patted my hat to make sure it was still in place.

"Oh, I got you something for the trip." He reached into his coat pocket. At first I thought it was a necklace, but it was a headlamp, the kind you take camping. He'd bought me a girlie one with a pink band and the white light dead center. I could walk around Seattle looking like a Cyclops. "It's always good to have a source of light, in case the power goes out, or whatnot. Better safe than sorry."

I thanked him and tucked it into my knapsack. My mind had been scoured of anything to say. Big dramatic moments were not my thing, but I still had those barnacles in my stomach. "Don't forget to turn the heat on sometimes," I added. "It's cold."

"I won't."

And with that, I handed my papers to the guard, was waved through, and entered the realm of Passengers Only.

There were a lot of gray- and white-haired people, along with a few couples trying to control young children. It was a sea of Gore-Tex jackets. There was an urn of coffee, and I watched the seniors flutter around it like pigeons. Verne would be halfway home by now, probably listening to CFAX radio to stay on top of news and weather. I pulled out my Discman and listened to a Mudhoney CD. *This is my mother's,* I thought, listening to *Every Good Boy Deserves Fudge.* The raw sounds calmed my nerves. Something was going to happen on this trip. I could feel it.

"Excuse me, miss, could you turn down that racket?"

I looked up, prepared to apologize, my usual strategy. A guy, maybe sixteen, was grinning at me, his face close to mine. He was obviously one of those people with no sense of personal space. He had a shaved head, which made his green eyes pop. There was a sprinkling of paprika freckles over his nose, making me think his hair was red. He was handsome.

"Excuse me?" I asked, lifting my headphones, squinting. I had no clue about how to flirt. I felt I had no goods to offer. I wore an A-cup. I would likely never be flabby, at least, because I walked. I walked like a speed-addicted postal worker. It was what I did.

"What are you listening to?" he asked. He looked like a ska guy. He had suspenders peeking out beneath his khaki parka. He was clearly like me, in a music time warp.

"Mudhoney," I half shouted, looking around. I hadn't been expecting a conversation.

"Well, that makes you the coolest girl in the room," he

said. "My name is Sean, by the way." He strolled back to his knapsack, which was army surplus. He'd written *The Jam* on it, a way-old ska band. Of course, no one listened to what I liked, either. Grunge was supposedly a cross of punk and heavy metal or something. I didn't like either alone, but together it was a perfect combination. It was the end of 2006, though, not 1992. Grunge was dead, or so I kept hearing.

When they finally let us on the ferry, everyone rushed to claim seats as if the last person standing had to drop their pants. I looked around dumbly. Already couples and families were spreading out magazines and coffee cups and video games. The seats were blue or red, all in banks of four or six, facing each other as if on a train.

I had wanted to catch glimpses of the dark sea boiling as we crossed, but the prime window seats were already taken by parties of four or five or six. Parties. If there were a few of you, it became a party. I had to sit somewhere; it was a two-and-a-half-hour trip. People were beginning to notice me standing there. One woman looked up from helping her daughter open a plastic tub filled with green grapes. Her eyes locked on mine; then she turned away. The little girl extracted one grape and popped it in her mouth. She didn't need to be greedy, since it was all for her. She wore a peach hairband and had two pigtails shooting out from either side of her head like spray from a garden hose. I wanted to gently tug on one of the girl's pigtails, as if pulling a cord to signal a train stop.

"Hey, Mudhoney, over here."

It was that guy, Sean, sitting in one of the banks of four, his long legs stretched out. I could feel my face getting hot. He made it sound like two words. Mud Honey.

"There's space here," he said, gesturing to the three seats, one of which was taken up with his army surplus bag.

Most of the free seats had been covered with bags or wet jackets. It was the best offer I would get. Sean was listening to something on his headphones and flashed me a smile. It didn't count as sitting next to a strange man. He wasn't quite a man yet, though he did seem strange, drumming his fingers on the armrest. The table had trays that folded out to make space if you wanted to eat or play cards. It would have been ideal for using the Ouija board.

If Sean didn't want to chitchat, that was fine. The two rejects were sitting together, which probably made everyone else feel comfortable. The ship started to move. There would be no turning back. My calf muscles unclenched.

"Do you have a shaved head?" Sean shouted at me, still listening to his headphones.

"No," I said. The answer seemed to satisfy him.

"Bummer," he muttered, crossing and uncrossing his legs at the ankle. He was one of those tall guys who appeared boneless. The people around me had settled down, drinking more coffee, talking, reading brochures about what to do in Seattle. I tried to guess which ones were returning home to Seattle and which were from Victoria. Middle-aged, middle-class Americans favored high-end, branded sportswear: ball caps with logos, jerseys, golf shirts, expensive sneakers with silver laces. It was as if wealthy Americans took everything seriously, even leisure time. They all seemed to be reading the same silver-and-blue paperback novel: *A Time to Cry* by Jasper Jameson. I patted my head, which was warm under the knit hat. I would have to rinse out the Kool-Aid at some point. Planning ahead was not one of my strengths, as guidance counselors often reminded me.

A young woman in a blue collared shirt was making the rounds of the ship, taking drink and snack orders. The plastic card on the table listed the options: various packs containing a hodgepodge of mini-snacks if your palate had ADHD and couldn't decide if it wanted crackers with cheese spread, dried cranberries, or salami. I settled on a packet of almonds and a Sprite. My small stature and my current waiflike appearance gave me a roughly 35 percent chance of being served a beer.

I opened my knapsack and rummaged through the CDs, settling upon *Incesticide*, the Nirvana compilation album first released in 1992. I had wanted it for weeks. My mother had owned it. I couldn't believe it. I had read that the album came out just after several singles from *Nevermind* were released, so the record company didn't give it heavy promotion. *Incesticide* contained "Sliver," the song about a boy visiting his grandparents' house when his parents go out—and he just wants to go home. It's simple kid-lyrics about bike riding and bashing your toe, and having trouble chewing meat, and wanting your mother. People tried to make a big deal about Cobain's lyrics and song titles, but sometimes they were just random, like "Sliver." The title had nothing to do with the song, and if you thought it did, the joke was on you.

The other song on the album I loved was "Dive," straight-ahead driving guitar. All the songs were simply produced, more punk and rough edges than what came later.

The *Incesticide* cover was artwork by Kurt Cobain featuring a skeletal figure with an oddly shaped doll clinging to its shoulder, and two flowers—one withered, one alive—by its wristbone. I shuddered, fascinated. There was something about dead flowers. While it was creepy, the skeleton was crouched in a kind of yoga pose, almost contemplative. The doll figure suggested . . . well, I didn't know. Hope? The back of the album showed a photo of a rubber duck, an item belonging to Cobain.

Sean was studying me. I smiled as if to say "Yeah?" I put my headphones back on and hit play. "Dive" started up, all searing and ominous. It seemed unlikely anyone would ever pick me, like the chorus said. I was never picked for anything, certainly not gym teams. I had stamina but was uncoordinated. I was clumsy. I tended to drop things.

While I listened, I thought that some people have the ability to bring a song to life, to sell it, to make you feel it. That's something Grandma Irene once said to me, talking about Frank Sinatra. I pulled out the liner notes, remembering that Cobain was credited on *Incesticide* as Kurdt Kobain, an alternate spelling he sometimes used.

As I unfolded the liner notes, a Polaroid fell out and fluttered to the floor. The photo was dark, aquatic, like a shark tank. Someone had written *The Forge, March 9, 1991* on the frame in blue marker. It took me only a second to realize: that someone was my mother. I felt my organs rearrange themselves and lurch back into place.

The photo was of Nirvana bassist Krist Novoselic playing a barefoot set in Victoria at the Forge, a bar since renamed and rebranded. To the right was Kurt Cobain, his blond hair covering his face, head down, focused on his guitar—his lifeline. The stop would have been a blip on their last tour before they went big, galactic, selling close to thirty million records. But there was someone else in the photo. I could see her velvet chestnut hair in the front row. She was half turning that beautiful aquiline nose to the camera, knowing her friend was pushing the button. Her face was blurry because she was dancing. She could be willing him to *pick me, pick me*. Would she have done that? She was quiet, introspective, but she could be a wild child, I'd heard. She was passionate about music. Kurt Cobain shared all those traits, it seemed to me. He knew all about dangerous feelings.

I held the Polaroid, forgetting where I was and who I was. The ship seemed to be spinning. I'd heard talk that Nirvana had played one show in Victoria, when they were largely unknown, before *Nevermind* took off like a supernova. One show. Only sixty or so people had been there. I pressed the Polaroid to my chest, as if it could stop my heart from flopping up and down. I thought I might do something crazy, like demand that the captain turn around or hurl myself overboard, anything to distract myself from the feelings I was having. My mother was at a Nirvana concert, *the* Nirvana concert. Concert promoters in Victoria still agonized over not booking that one.

I placed the photo facedown on my thigh and extracted my laptop from my knapsack. My legs were trembling, making the screen shake. Ten seconds later the set list for Nirvana, the Forge, March 9, 1991, popped up. I had saved it as a PDF during one of my late-night Internet sessions. The band opened with a cover of "Love Buzz" by Shocking Blue, probably roaring onto the stage. They followed with "Sliver" and "Dive." I closed my eyes for a second to let it all sink in. My mother loved Nirvana. She'd stood just a few feet away from Kurt Cobain. She maybe even touched him.

I plugged my headphones into my CD player and listened to "Sliver," trying to imagine Annalee's face as she heard it, how she danced. Aunt Gillian had once told me, "Your mother liked to go a little wild," but I didn't know what that meant. Grandma Irene thought flavored coffee beans were wild. Verne was much the same. I suspected Aunt Gillian could let loose, but not in front of her underage niece. I also sometimes thought my aunt was a lesbian but that no one had bothered to tell me yet.

Sean drummed his fingers so hard on the table that I could feel the vibrations. Was he trying to bug me? Now he was drinking a beer he had managed to obtain, even though I was sure he wasn't legal. He tapped the bottle, asking.

Yeah, I wanted some. I nodded. He smiled, looked to see if anyone was watching, then poured half his beer into a plastic cup. He passed it to me with a big grin. I downed it in one gulp. Sean raised his auburn eyebrows. The beer, flat as it was, tasted good. One more and I'd be ready to face my future. I smiled at Sean. Then I dug around for another CD from my mother's collection. It would be her copy of *Bleach*, the first Nirvana album. It was recorded for $606.17, and the band members, who were sick at the time, drank a lot of cough syrup. I gave Sean the thumbs-up while keeping my headphones on. I was trying to ignore how cute he was.

Somehow, my mother and I had found the same music. Maybe four out of five therapists would say I'd subconsciously searched out the music from her time; what did it matter? We'd landed in the same place. The Polaroid rested on my leg, under my hand. I'd clamped it there as if I'd trapped a moth to be carried outside. Her camera must have been vintage, even then. I lifted up the photo. It felt thick, so I picked at the bottom with my thumbnail. I uncovered another photo stuck to the first, equally grainy. This one showed a microphone, a stage light, and a man's hand reaching out. Then there was my mother's profile: the sloping nose, her flawless teeth. There was her hand, the hand of a young, beautiful girl, Annalee, also reaching out. Reaching out to Kurt Cobain.

I stopped the CD so I could just sit and stare at the photo. The noise of the ship filled my ears: the children squabbling, adults getting boisterous on the beer or wine, people becoming animated by the excitement of drawing closer or getting farther away from home.

In the photo, Cobain's hair is cut just short of his jawline. It is a moon-white blond. He wears a dark sweatshirt. His mouth is just over the microphone. Annalee would have been the most beautiful girl in the club. She always was, to hear my aunt talk. The photos I have seen (and memorized) show a young woman who liked to wear beaded necklaces and gazed at the camera shyly behind her long lashes, as if keeping a secret. My favorite photo of the two of us was taken at a local park when I was almost three. In it, my mother is holding me up in the air like a prize she has just won. I'm wearing a white cardigan over a yellow dress with white ankle socks and pink shoes. She has clipped tiny butterfly barrettes into my wispy white hair. We're both smiling. I don't remember the day it was taken. It is not one of my memories.

Verne confirmed my mother's beauty, though he could provide no great details, as if Annalee were an old hope chest that he could not bear to open, its contents left unexamined. The attic. Was it possible there were more boxes of her belongings? By 1991, the year of the concert, Annalee would have been dating Verne, who at the time was taking college courses, working as a security guard, and also sometimes driving a truck delivering frozen foods to various institutions in Greater Victoria, old-age homes and the like. When work ethic was being handed out, Verne got in line twice.

The bar where the concert was held, the Forge, would have been filled with smoke, though Annalee shunned cigarettes. She did occasionally enjoy a drink called a snakebite, a mix of cider and lager. Perhaps that stemmed from her British heritage. I had vowed to order one someday. *The lady will have a snakebite.*

A child began screaming, "I had it! I had it!" It was seven p.m. I felt like screaming the same words, for there was a thought dragging into my head, hopping on crutches into my consciousness. I had memorized a card catalog of details about Kurt Cobain: How he loved strawberry milk, just like me. How he was small and thin, just like me, and was obsessed with art.

A woman across from me wearing shiny red boots had doused herself in drugstore perfume. It was hard to breathe. She was clearly a shopper, with shiny red nails that matched her boots, her faux-fur-trimmed vest and leather bag. You could tell a person's style by the quality of their bag. Mine was a hand-me-down knapsack with a yellow button on it that read *I Love Nanaimo*, which I thought was funny, because *love* seemed like a pretty strong word when it came to Nanaimo, a city up Vancouver Island that was famous for its annual bathtub race.

Rummaging in my grubby knapsack, I finally found the CD of *Bleach*. It was their debut, which sounds so fresh and hopeful—the way I was supposed to feel at my age. Kurt Cobain named the album after seeing an AIDS prevention sign warning drug users to "Bleach your works." I had been putting off listening to it, her copy. I had been saving it, even though I already knew every song.

The third song on it is "About a Girl," which Cobain wrote after listening to the Beatles all day, and some critics say it's one of his finest songs. It was amazing that I'd finished school that term. I'd read about Kurt Cobain obsessively, and the Internet always had more, offering up millions of hits. You could spend hours trying to decide on his brand of cigarettes or his sexual preferences, let alone whether he was murdered.

I turned the album over and stared at it closely, realizing it was different from mine. There was writing on it, scratched in soft green pencil: *For Annalee, Kurt Cobain.* I stared, thinking the letters would disappear. The *K* looked as if it were kicking the *U*. The C looped. There was a bent peace sign scrawled at the bottom. I tried to explain it away. Perhaps her girlfriend had scrawled it as a joke. I knew she'd had a good friend, Janey, who'd moved away just after I was born.

I raised myself up on Bambi legs, bumping into tables on my way to the bathroom. I banged my hipbone on the sink in the coffin-sized washroom. After peeing for what seemed like several minutes, I washed my hands with the Barbie-pink soap from the dispenser, then stuck my head under the tap under the tiny sink. It was time. I undid the plastic wrap and tossed it in the garbage next to an orange peel and a disposable diaper. I felt a head rush as I straightened up, my hair now smelling like pink public bathroom soap instead of sweet fruit. Scrubbing my head with the paper towel made the paper fiber disintegrate in my hair. I shook my head, spraying droplets on the mirror.

My hair in the white fluorescent light was teal, almost jade, falling just to my jawline. My hair was the color of a snow cone. Tucking a strand behind my ear, I didn't recognize the girl in the mirror: She was smiling. Heads turned as I strode back to my seat, or so I imagined. If Sean was surprised he didn't show it, giving me one brisk nod.

He studied me a moment, then pulled off his headphones.

"Wow," said Sean. "You didn't tell me you were so cute."

My cheeks glowed like a burner on high.

"Needed a change," I mumbled.

Sean seemed to take this response as an invitation. He moved over to take the seat next to me. I didn't mind. "What are you doing in Seattle?" he asked.

"Visiting my aunt. She's a nurse."

"Where 'bouts?" he asked. The way he said it made me think he was Canadian.

"She has a condo in Belltown." Why was I telling him this? I was breaking every rule about strange young men.

"You live in Victoria? Do a lot of chicks there have blue hair?"

"Yeah, and yeah. But in Victoria it's the old ladies."

"My older brother is working there at the Empress Hotel, so I went to visit him. We've got dual citizenship 'cause of my mom."

I bristled at the word *mom*, as I sometimes did. You'd think I would be used to being motherless, but you'd be wrong. Until I knew what happened to her, I would always be waiting. Every time the mail arrived. Every time the phone rang. Just thinking about her made me want to fill my head with Nirvana. I knew other kids who'd had a parent take off, deadbeat dads and all that, but none of them had just disappeared.

"I'll take you there, if you want," Sean was saying. He looked at me sideways, kind of shy all of a sudden.

"Sorry, take me where?"

"The Space Needle. Then Pike Place Market. We can get tattoos." He smiled and tapped his Doc Martens again.

"You don't even know my name."

"What's your name?" he asked. "Or I could just call you Blue."

"Nico."

"Pleased to meet you."

"Sean, how old are you?"

"Just turned sixteen. But I have ID, courtesy of my brother. Best not to ask too many questions."

"Wow," I said. "Score." Effective fake ID was the holy grail of high school. You could move up several rungs on the social ladder if you had ID. It was better than having clueless parents with a big liquor cabinet or being a kick-ass drummer.

"So, seriously, I don't live that far from downtown. I could be your tour guide."

"Yeah, m-maybe," I stuttered. It seemed unlikely my aunt would go for that, but she'd be at the hospital during the day. She didn't have to know. It was a revelation. I had Smurf-blue hair. Anything could happen. I felt a surge of something go through me, a cold stream of happiness.

"What are you listening to?" He nodded at my Disc-man, which had been fine three years ago but was now clunky and outdated. Verne had gotten it for me second-hand or something. He didn't like to acknowledge that we had trouble affording extras. We had never gone to a food bank, true, but I'd worn a lot of consignment-store rain boots and eaten a plantation's worth of peanut butter.

"Nirvana," I said, looking at his eyes, which were a watery green. I had vowed to stop being hesitant about my retro taste in music. During a year that saw the lame anthem "Bad Day" top the charts, there was no shame. "You?"

"The Skatalites."

I nodded. Obe had one of their discs. It was too boppy for me, but it showed that Sean listened outside the mainstream. And Nirvana was no longer mainstream, not in my world. Sure, roofers would sing along to "Smells Like Teen Spirit" while listening to the classic-rock radio station, but being obsessed with those old bands wasn't exactly cool at Vic High. Nirvana was something your parents used to like. Kurt Cobain, on the other hand, had retained his cool by his grand exit through the greenhouse. He never got old.

"My mother loved Nirvana," I blurted out.

Why was I such an idiot? I never mentioned my mother.

"Cool. My mother loves Garth Brooks. There's always a Garth album in the car. It gives me hives, Nico, actual hives."

We were only about a half hour from Seattle. Some of the children had fallen asleep. Adults had finished sharing bottles of wine and were bleary-eyed and subdued.

"I could probably meet you after my aunt goes to work,"

I said, surprised at my own boldness. I hadn't even begun to think about how Aunt Gillian would react to my blue hair, or if she'd call Verne.

He wrote a number down on a Clipper flyer that listed duty-free items.

"Give me a call. I live in Bellevue, but I'm usually downtown. I work part-time at the Armory."

I frowned. He was in the military?

"It's a kind of historic mall, near Seattle Center."

I nodded. I had a strong urge to email Obe. I could make it one word: *BOY!* Obe would guess what I meant, or close to it.

Sean had big shoulders, a solid-looking chest under his white T-shirt. He was closer to being a man than the reedy, artsy boys I always crushed on. My targets typically had piercings and a tendency to wear monochrome clothes, like Brit-accent Bryan did. The one thing they usually had in common: a lack of burning interest in Nico Cavan.

Sean and I traded Discmans for the last few minutes of the ferry ride, switching back just as we landed. The ska made me jittery and awake. There was a boy who seemed interested in me. My mother had gone to see Nirvana and practically held hands with Kurt Cobain. My hair was blue. A lot had happened in three hours. Suddenly, I was starving.

I lost Sean in the crush to get off the ferry. Standing in line to go through customs, I felt scattered, withering under the frowns of seniors who didn't care for my teal hair. The whole room smelled like wet luggage and the sweet lily perfume favored by old ladies. The ferry terminal resembled a cattle pen rather than a gateway to international fun, despite the posters advertising the Undersea Gardens and the Empress Hotel in Victoria.

The border guard did a double-take, looking at my passport, my hair, and my passport again. I should have put my hat back on, but I had forgotten. The man had thick eyebrows, like two black caterpillars. He asked me several questions about my aunt and then asked to see my passport again. I repeated when I expected to return.

"I'm fifteen. A student in high school." Hadn't I already mentioned that? He seemed convinced that I wanted to stay in America. No thanks. Not until they got rid of President Bush.

"Okay, Nicola Cavan. Welcome to Seattle," he said, and slapped my passport closed. Dazed, I picked up my packs and swung them on. My knapsack was lumpy and heavy, stuffed with CDs. As I staggered into the terminal, I heard shrieking.

"Nico! YOUR HAIR!"

Then Gillian was upon me, holding my face, kissing my cheeks. She was wearing a newsboy-type cap over her auburn curls, and a frosted peach lipstick, both of which made her look a decade younger than her thirty-eight years. Gillian worked at happiness like a job, refusing to let things get her down. She was a kick-ass nurse on staff at Virginia Mason Medical Center, one of the top hospitals. She'd had to take all these tests to get her license in the States, but she'd said it was worth it for the challenges and better pay. I'd wondered if there was more to it, if she was seeing someone in Seattle, but if there was, she never told me. She always said she'd come back to Canada one day.

"What does my big brother think about this?" she asked, tugging on my hair. Gillian is loud, perhaps from all the years of chaos at the hospital.

"He doesn't know," I said, and laughed, because she was laughing. It was almost impossible not to laugh when Gillian did.

"Did you eat, girlie girl?" she asked, putting her hand on my shoulder to steer me to the parking lot.

"I had a snackette."

"I don't do snackettes," she said as we neared her car, a new-model yellow Volkswagen Beetle. "Let's stop for some takeout Thai on the way home."

I put my slicker hood over my hair against the cold rain. In the rain Olympics, Seattle would take gold, even against Victoria. Gillian said she gave up on flat-ironing her hair when she moved there, but I can't imagine her ever having the patience to use one of those contraptions.

She opened the door for me, and I got into the passenger side. My body sighed, the way it does at the end of a journey. Gillian started the car, and I leaned my head back. I watched the raindrops race each other down the window like I did when I was little, listening to the windshield wipers mutter back and forth. Something, or someone, was coming my way. I could feel it.

CHAPTER 6

"THE MAN WHO SOLD THE WORLD"

While we ate dinner, Gillian kept sneaking looks at my hair. "I shouldn't admit this, but I like it," she said gleefully, scraping her plate for the last of her rice. Her Fourth Avenue condo was only six hundred or so square feet, and it was jammed with belongings. Her condo was everything my house wasn't: new, bright, and owned. There were a lap pool and a fitness room downstairs, complete with sauna. She sometimes had four days off at a time, so she had lots of hobbies. She worked her twelve-hour shifts and then she played hard.

Gillian had already asked me about boys, my grades, my plans for the future (same vague answer as always, "art school"), and how Obe was doing. ("Obe is Obe.")

"Nothing new, Nico?" She looked at me.

"New?" She couldn't know about Sean, or the albums. Had Gillian known about the box?

"Sweetie bun, I meant on the case." She sighed and stood to clear the kitchen table, which was a stylish glass-topped egg shape just big enough for two.

"No, nothing," I said. "Or if there is, no one's told me." The file was technically open, but there'd been no rumblings for two years. Back then, someone with her name got a speeding ticket in the town of Hope, BC, of all places. False alarm. Next year it would be more than a decade since she'd been gone. I knew no one thought she was alive. Perhaps Gillian wondered when I would stop living in suspended animation, or whatever I was doing.

Gillian had set up the sofa bed in her office for me. She had fresh, Granny Smith–colored bedding, abstract art prints on the wall. The office window faced the street, which I remembered could be noisy. She was right in the heart of the action in Belltown, near Seattle Center and the Space Needle, which I had never been up, not yet.

I paged through the Kurt Cobain book Obe had given me. I had read several biographies in a row, and the effect was of having eaten too much, too quickly. All the facts about Cobain's life were popcorning in my head.

Kurt's parents were working-class poor. His mother, Wendy, was a blond beauty. Donald was a mechanic. They married young. When Kurt was born, even the nurses in the hospital commented on his beautiful blue eyes. He was a happy kid until his parents split up, and then they fought, and hated each other, and everything changed forever. His parents thought he had ADHD, so they gave him Ritalin. He later said that might have set the stage for his drug use. His wife, Courtney, who was also drugged as a kid, said the same thing. But I didn't want to think about her.

When Kurt Cobain was a teenager, some people might have thought he was lazy. For one thing, he didn't do well in school, except art. But later he was a janitor and did crap jobs just to make enough money for Nirvana's first demo. When he really smiled, he had a grin as wide and bright as a crescent moon. He hated to brush his teeth. He loved playing his guitar. He had an encyclopedic knowledge of pop and rock. He could play for hours and didn't mind if he was grounded because he loved to sit in his room with his guitar.

As a teen, he was shuffled from one house to another, even staying with his grandparents and a high school teacher. He said he once slept under a bridge in Aberdeen, which he wrote about in "Something in the Way." Some people say he exaggerated all that and lots of other stories of his past, but he was a storyteller. That's what they do. He had a thing for thrift stores.

His first serious girlfriend, Tracy Marander, heard about him as the kid who drew cartoons of the rock group Kiss on the side of the Melvins' van, "the Melvan," as it was known. The Melvins were a punk rock group that Kurt idolized after hearing them play at a grocery store parking lot or something.

Kurt drew all his life. When he was small he was accused

of copying a cartoon of Donald Duck—but he hadn't. He was just good. In high school, he drew a sketch of two aging punk rockers with piercings, evoking *American Gothic*, that famous painting of the old lady with the bun and the dude with the pitchfork. One of his collages became the album art for *In Utero*. When he was photographing the collage, his baby daughter, Frances Bean, kept trying to play with the materials. If I ever met Frances Bean, we would have something in common: having only one parent. Except she would be a millionaire when she was older, something I wouldn't have to worry about.

Gillian knocked on the door. I was going to try to hide the book, but that would look even more suspicious.

"Oh," said Gillian, noticing the cover, which was the black-and-white portrait of Kurt Cobain. "Why are you reading that?" Her mouth turned down. Dozens of teens had committed suicide after hearing about the discovery of Cobain's body on April 8, 1994. He was a personal hero to them, a rock god. Perhaps she thought I would revive the trend. Some Canadian teens drove across the country and committed suicide together in a storage unit in Langley, not far from Vancouver. They died from carbon monoxide poisoning. The police found Nirvana cassette tapes on the scene, and in a journal one of the young men had written that when Kurt Cobain died, he did too.

"Aunt Gillian, I just like their music. I know my mom did, too."

"Oh," she said, sitting on the edge of the sofa bed. I was glad I was wearing the little floral pajamas Grandma

Irene had given me instead of, say, a T-shirt that read *The Screaming Trees*.

She thought for a moment. "How did you find that out?"

"I found a box of her albums and stuff. They'd been at Grandma Irene's."

Gillian turned to the window, though the blinds were closed.

"I think your dad planned to give those to you when you were older. He thought they made your mom sad."

So Gillian knew, too. Everyone knew. There was no one I could trust.

"Maybe Verne made my mom sad."

"That's possible, too. But, Nico . . ."

"Clearly." I thought I might cry like a kid who'd dropped an ice cream cone. I was sure they'd gotten married because my mother was pregnant with me. No one had ever spelled it out, but it seemed obvious.

"There are things you don't know, Nico."

"There are things he should have told me."

"What are you going to do tomorrow?" she asked, stroking my hair. "Still getting used to the blue."

"I thought I would go to the science center," I said, not sure if I was lying. Maybe we would go there. "Then to the Armory."

"Have a good sleep, my sweet little Smurf," said Gillian, kissing my cheek.

"Good night, Aunt Gillian," I said.

After she left and gently closed the door, I thought about what she'd said: *There are things you don't know, Nico.*

The sofa bed was soft and firm at the same time. My aunt had good taste and a knack for selecting things like furniture and linen. I rested my head and read more about Kurt Cobain, or Kurdt Kobain, the man who wanted to be a rock star but hated celebrity. The man of a thousand contradictions.

CHAPTER 7

"DIVE"

I was alone in my house all the time, but somehow in Gillian's condo it was different, more relaxing. For one, I knew it had a security system where you had to be buzzed in, as well as hidden cameras and two locks on the door. At our place, I was always worried someone would break in, some junkie looking to grab a few things.

Gillian had left me a note on the kitchen table. *Coffee beans in freezer, yogurt, bagels, you know what to do. See you at 7:30 for dinner, then I'm FREE!*

I couldn't imagine doing anything for twelve hours except sleeping. Certainly not a job. Maybe I could draw that long, but that wasn't a real job. I stood in Gillian's shiny kitchen and set about making myself fresh-ground coffee. While I was waiting for the french press to steep, I put on my mother's copy of *Nevermind*. I let it play through, occasionally patting my blue hair, enjoying being in my pajamas and reading more about Cobain. Starting on my third cup of coffee, I decided to do a sketch of Gillian to surprise her. After that, I would call Sean. The music stopped, and the condo was strangely silent, something I was not used to. Our Victoria neighborhood was noisy, whether it was rowdies yelling in the street or the old lady who lived downstairs and cranked the television news. Quiet was unnerving. It got you thinking.

Then there was a noise on the stereo like raccoons fighting. My heart jumped, and I realized it was the beginning of "Endless, Nameless," a caterwauling of a song. I listened, transfixed, almost scared.

My mother loved Nirvana, early, before everyone else in the world did. Was she angry, even then? Or did she just love music? My questions pressed on my chest, squeezing out the air.

I lay on Gillian's couch, listening to the hidden track, and remembered I had promised to call Sean. He had probably forgotten about me. When "Endless, Nameless" was over, I picked up the phone.

When you wear thrift-store clothes there's a fine line between being charmingly different and looking like you dressed from a lost-and-found bin. I had no one to dish out fashion advice, so I wore a secondhand floral dress with black leggings. I clipped my hair back with a silver barrette, which Gillian said made me look pretty because it showed the angular cheekbones I had inherited from my mother.

I was to meet Sean at the Armory after his shift at the coffee shop, which he admitted was part of a big chain that exploited its workers. I didn't mind. Money was money. Now that I was fifteen, I planned to try to get a part-time job so I wouldn't have to ask Verne for cash.

Leaving Gillian's building and walking on my own in a strange city, it was almost as if something was falling off me, cracking, the way they say glaciers groan when they separate.

I saw Sean before he noticed me. He was watching some old man play his guitar in front of the Armory. The man played "Jesus Loves Me" while a fuzzy-haired woman and her two children sang along and tapped their feet. Sean stood there, a big grin on his face. The young mother swung one of the boys between her feet as they all sang. The other one mumbled something.

"We've got rice cakes in the bag, Ethan, don't you worry," she assured her boy, who was probably two or three. The other appeared to be almost school age, maybe four. They had identical crew cuts, as if their mother had buzzed them with a razor. Easy peasy, lemon squeezy. Who had said that to me?

The man singing wore a gray suit and a fedora; he was the picture of a bluesman. He was busking for coins, but he was calm and self-assured. The song ended and the kids gave the singer sloppy high-fives, and the mother put two green U.S. dollars into the man's guitar case. Sean saw me and waved. Someone, for once, was expecting me.

"Nico," he said, smiling. "Do you need a coffee before we head out?"

How did people learn to be that way? So easy, so welcoming. He touched me lightly on the shoulder and my pulse shot up.

"No, thanks, I had some at my aunt's place."

"What would you like to do first?"

Go somewhere warm, I thought, wishing I'd put on another layer under my jacket. I hadn't wanted to look chunky. Vanity would cost me. Damp cold was the worst.

"How about the science center?" I asked. He pulled his gray hood over his head against the cold drizzle. Why was he wasting time on me? If he knew how ignored I was back in Victoria, he would never be seen with me.

"Okay, Mud Honey, let's go." He grabbed my hand. I let out a laugh that was somewhere between surprise and delight.

There was a butterfly on me. I could feel it trembling. Somehow the idea of something so delicate and fine on my body made me panic. It could be killed so easily. We had been told before entering the tropical butterfly house that if one landed on us, we should just gently shake our clothes.

Sean leaned forward and gave the sleeve of my dress a slight tug. The butterfly, a blue Morpho, veered off, flying in its dizzying pattern, as if a puppeteer were manipulating its wings with strings. I loved Morphos. I had never seen one so close before. Maybe I liked them because I was blue now, too.

We headed to the double doors. Beyond them, there was an enclosed area where we checked each other for butterflies. They had to be kept in the tropical house, where they would be given fruit and nectar. Sean and I were alone. There was quiet. Soft. A family barged in at that moment, including twin boys in ball caps who couldn't stop fighting. Loud. The spell was broken. Sean ushered me out, making sure no butterflies followed us. In the warmth of the tropical house I had looked up at the ceiling and regretted it, because there were all these dead butterflies trapped in the lights. They had tried to get away, to soar out, but the chilly Seattle winter would have killed them on the spot. Either way, they had flown to their deaths.

"Let's go see the show at the planetarium," Sean said. He seemed to know when to talk and when to be quiet. I think he knew, even on the ferry, that there was something strange about me, not just my weird hair or my outdated plaid flannel shirt. Perhaps he found me intriguing, the way you puzzle over someone with one gray eye and one blue, until you figure out what's different.

I had told Sean about Verne but hadn't mentioned my mother, and he hadn't asked. He lived with both his parents, but his father traveled a lot (something to do with e-commerce that I didn't fully get). He had an older sister in first year at university who seemed to have temporarily forgotten about her family, which made his mother hysterical. There was his brother, too; he worked in the kitchen at the Empress and was a jokester. Sean seemed close to him.

Usually when I went to places that were packed with families and grandparents and strollers, I felt lonely, but not that day. I was curious to know what Sean saw in me, an un-girlie Canadian girl. I snorted to myself, sending a laugh up my nasal passages.

"Are planetariums funny in Canada? Here they tend to be pretty serious," he said as we waited in line for the show. I just smiled back at him.

There were only a few other people in the planetarium once we got in. I liked the feeling, dark and safe, like a warm cave. Sean's shoulder was almost touching mine, and I felt my skin buzzing, as if a Morpho had landed there. I wondered if he would take my hand again.

A fellow with a booming voice and saucer-sized glasses was trying too hard to keep the little kids in the room awake by being overly animated as he talked about Orion, the Big Dipper, Ursa Major and Ursa Minor, Draco the dragon. As the lights darted above my head, I got sleepy, as if someone had given me a potion. I woke up with my head on Sean's shoulder. The children and their parents were shuffling out, and Sean had a slight smile on his face, his green eyes curious. So much for playing it cool. I removed my head from his shoulder. The presenter, who had one of those midlife-crisis ponytails that look like a squirrel pelt, shuffled his paper star guides, no doubt annoyed. At least the children had stayed awake.

"Sorry," I said. "Guess I'm still tired from exams." That was only partially true. I was tired from staying up all night listening to Nirvana tracks online and reading articles about Kurt Cobain, clicking on photo galleries, videos, fan sites. The hits were as infinite as the galaxy. I had once thought about buying Cobain's published journals. *If you read, you'll judge*, it said on the cover, which was a mockup of a red Mead spiral notebook. It seemed wrong to read the journals. It would be like spying on someone undressing. But I'd read almost anything on the websites, with all their bad grammar, trash talk, and dubious conspiracy theories.

"How about a trip to Pike Place Market? That will blow your mind," said Sean.

I had been to the market once before, but I had a feeling it would be different with Sean. I knew there was no way anyone would want me running around Seattle with a boy I barely knew, charming green eyes or no. Getting on a bus with him seemed like a big step, for some reason. It was like doing a stage dive.

"Let's go," I said, shoving my hands in my pockets. My blue hair spilled from my ponytail in a way that I hoped looked appealing. On the bus, he asked what I wanted to be when I grew up. He said it in a silly way, mocking all the adults who ask, hoping you'll say something they understand, like doctor or tax attorney. I was fixated on our fellow passengers. A few rows away one woman was shouting to another: "I was trying to help you out, bitch!"

Seattle seemed to have more rough edges than Victoria. But I didn't mind rough edges. They were better than lies.

"An artist," I said. I had never admitted that to anyone before. "I wish I could play guitar."

"Does anyone in your family play?" he asked.

"No. I don't think so," I said.

The two women at the front of the bus began screaming at each other. One had thought the other was sleeping and tried to wake her up.

"Driver!" shrieked one of them. She had big hair, piled up like a copper layer cake, and shiny silver earrings. "This woman is harassing me!"

Sean rolled his eyes. The driver ignored the commotion. The second woman, wearing a New Age–y quilted coat with half moons on it, changed seats, moving farther down the bus.

Sean held his face close to mine, as if we were separated by glass and I were a peculiar animal he was trying to figure out.

"I don't know my mother," I said. "She left when I was four. She loved music. She liked hiking. She sang. I don't really know." The last few words I think I said to myself. The bus was suddenly quiet, everyone straining to hear if the women's dispute would resume.

"Oh, Nico," he said. "That's really rough."

I had done it. Now he felt sorry for me, like everyone else.

"Every day I wonder where she is," I said, my voice even and flat. "I wonder if she's alive. Why she left me."

"Of course you do," he said, and then he put his arm around me. He was wearing soft fleece gloves. "I'll bet she was beautiful, just like you."

She was beautiful. I knew that for sure. Oh my God. He had said I was beautiful.

"Maybe tomorrow we could go to the Experience Music Project Museum," he said. "Since you like music so much."

We. Tomorrow.

"I don't know how I can get away from my aunt. She's going to want to spend the whole day with me. I'm not sure she'd approve of you."

He shrugged. "Parents love me."

"She's not a parent."

I felt better after I told him about my mother. When I kept her a secret, it made me feel as if my stomach was filled with icicles. The therapists I had seen over the years all told me the same thing: none of it was my fault. But sometimes it seemed to me that everything was, as Nirvana declared in "All Apologies." What kind of person has their mother just disappear?

"Can we go see the Crocodile Café?" I asked Sean.

"Sure," he said, as if expecting the request. As we headed toward Pike Place, I was almost jogging. Sean had long legs, and I was trying to take everything in. One of those odd hybrids of boat and bus blasted past, with the tourists on board all singing a Christmas carol as their guide conducted them. A homeless man on the corner "raised the roof" in response, pushing his hands up in the air. I had forgotten it was almost Christmas, or at least, I had tried.

Cold rain verging on sleet was firing down from the sky. I knew the market would be crowded, colorful, packed with stands carrying strange produce like star fruit, comic book stores, diners overlooking the gray expanse of Puget Sound. Sean would want to show me the novelty store with all the retro posters, the cardboard cutouts of pop culture icons like R2-D2 or the cast of *Battlestar Galactica*. Visiting the market as a girl, I had searched out the candy stores.

We approached the entrance, and I could hear the fishmongers yelling, doing some kind of performance that was their claim to fame. As we neared the crowd, Sean held out his hand.

CHAPTER 8

"LOVE BUZZ"

Near the end of the video for "Heart-Shaped Box," a breeze blows a white peaked cap off the head of a spooky little blond girl with enormous blue eyes. That's the song where Kurt Cobain sings that when you turned black, he wished he could eat your cancer.

A wave of blue butterflies drifts across the screen. The white cap soars after them. The cap lands in a black puddle and quickly soaks it up until it has completely turned black. I had forgotten about the blue butterflies.

I was recalling that, and eating a grilled-cheese sandwich, when Sean asked what I was thinking about. He had taken me to the 5 Point Cafe, which he claimed had the best diner food in town. It had longevity, for sure, with the slogan "Alcoholics serving alcoholics since 1929." It was close to my aunt's place, but I had never been there. I loved it.

"I was thinking this is a really good grilled cheese," I said. "Thanks for bringing me here." The place had been voted Seattle's best dive bar and best diner.

"Of course," he said, taking a bite of his hamburger. The fries at the place were massive and plentiful, piled up like kindling.

Sean chatted easily about his parents. His dad was into gadgets and watching sports on television; his mother liked country music and was obsessed with yoga. His older sister would one day attend his wedding, be an aunt to his children. He had his older brother, who let him stay at his place in Victoria. He'd need the fingers of both hands to count the people who loved him.

"What do you want to be when you grow up?" I asked him. A man in a brown knit hat at the bar was getting drunker by the minute. The restaurant had an adults-only side and a diner side. We were on the diner side since I was underage (and so was Sean, technically). The man kept ordering something called a red eye, which Sean said was beer and tomato juice. Disgusting.

There was also a group of university kids and an older couple in nice clothes: strand of pearls for the lady, tie for the man. The 5 Point had a varied clientele.

"A reporter," he said, without hesitation. "I'm nosy. I like stories. Ideally I'd cover music or sports, but crime holds a certain appeal."

"Oh yeah? What sports teams do you follow?"

"Seattle Sonics, for one, but I'm preparing to have my heart broken by them."

The drunk talked loudly about a job interview he'd just had. Apparently he was from Olympia, the town where Kurt Cobain had ended up after high school; he'd lived in a house on Pear Street. I retained these details, just like the girl with the quart of milk and the stick of butter.

"Nico," Sean was saying. "Do you like basketball?"

I kept having mini-blackouts thinking about Kurt Cobain and Nirvana. I almost expected Kurt Cobain to walk into the diner and demand a hamburger. Maybe it was being in Seattle, where people erroneously thought the Nirvana sound developed. The whole grunge scene was marketed around Seattle in the 1990s, though. That was when the fashion magazines packaged plaid shirts and knit hats as the "grunge look" on the runways.

"Yeah. But I'm too small to be any good. So what made you want to be my tour guide today?" I asked, surprised at my own boldness.

"I think you're cute," he said. "And you look like you need a friend."

I smiled. No one had thought I was cute for about eight years. I was used to hearing I looked sad. "Ya look like your dog just died!" a man in a pickup shouted at me once, then sped away.

"Have you ever been to Aberdeen?" I asked.

"It's a real shithole," he said. "But yeah, it's where Kurt Cobain grew up. What did you think of the Crocodile?"

I shrugged. I had tried to picture Nirvana playing there. It was like any other dive club, but seedier, with more charisma. It had a big green sign that resembled scales. A lot of great bands had played there: Nirvana, R.E.M., Mudhoney, Pearl Jam. Kurt Cobain hated Pearl Jam. It wasn't easy being a musician, it seemed. For example, some music critics said *Bleach*, Nirvana's first and most punk album, was too simple, but then complained that *Nevermind* was overproduced. I liked them both.

"Maybe I'll become a total Canadian," said Sean, taking a long sip of his Coke. "The Bush clan is driving me mental. At least your head of state isn't *coco loco*."

"Not like Bush, anyway," I said. I was still thinking about this young couple having a rabid fight in front of the Crocodile, which had been closed. The girl had ink-black hair and a red kerchief, black eyeliner, red lipstick. The guy was in a black motorcycle jacket. Seattle liked black. The argument was getting heated, something about coming in late, insulting a sister, and a cat left unfed—all in one. Sean and I had shuffled along, embarrassed. You could practically feel the intensity radiating off them as they argued. I blushed, wondering if they would have make-up sex later.

"So what do you say, Nico? Do you want to get married so I can become a full-on Canadian?"

He gave me a lazy smile. He chewed on his straw. He was not nearly as charming as he thought he was. Well, maybe he was.

"Yeah . . . no," I said, then thought of Obe. He hated when people said that. "Not today, anyway. I've got to meet my aunt in under an hour, and she wouldn't like me hanging out all day with a strange guy, let alone marrying one."

"I'm not strange!" he huffed. "Do you want to see the periscope in the men's room before we go?"

He accidentally dropped a pocketful of change on the floor and then paid for my lunch over my objections, which was sweet and made me suspicious at the same time. It seemed absurd that Obe didn't know about this guy yet. Obe knew almost everything about me, except how sad I could be sometimes.

"Your dress is really cool," Sean said, tugging on the sleeve. I felt a chill race down my arms. The dress, which had cost four dollars at Value Village, was navy cotton with tiny pink and white flowers and appeared to be handmade. We ducked out as the drunk was embarking on a long story about a baseball game. "When do you leave?" he asked.

"Day after tomorrow. Christmas Eve." He thought I was cool. He wasn't making fun of me. Nobody thought I was cool, except maybe Obe.

"Back to your dad?"

"Yeah," I said. Verne seemed very far away. He had already phoned Gillian to make sure I had arrived safely. She'd said I was sleeping, though I was listening to another one of my mother's CDs and reading the Cobain bio by flashlight.

"Do you like anything more mellow than Nirvana and the Pixies?" Sean asked.

"'Redemption Song' by Bob Marley," I told him, which

was true. There was something about the opening chords. And the words: the idea that you could suffer but endure.

"Noted. Maybe next time I come to Victoria we can hang out," he said as we walked toward my aunt's place on Fourth. The wind had picked up, and strands of my blue hair whipped across my face. Breaking with my no-makeup custom, I had worn mascara and charcoal eyeliner, hoping I looked like a young Chrissie Hynde—the eyes, anyway.

Something skittered in my stomach. Excitement. Nerves. One thing I knew: I didn't want to go home. I didn't want to be abandoned Nicola Irene Cavan with the dishwater-blond hair, and the sad dad, and the reckless young mother who had disappeared. The new, blue-haired Nico with the vintage CD collection seemed to be appealing to boys, decisive, and even slightly opinionated.

I formed my hands into two bundles, squeezing my fingers, which were clumsy with cold. I slapped them against my legs to warm them, making a thrumming sound like a bass line. One of Kurt Cobain's first real high school friends was bass player Krist Novoselic. He was a giant. Kurt and Krist formed a band and they sometimes practiced above a hair salon owned by Krist's mother. They were two freaks in Aberdeen, a less than scenic logging town packed with bars with names like the Pourhouse.

I felt a hand wrap around mine. It was Sean's.

"So am I going to see you tomorrow?" he asked as we started to cross the street. Sean stopped in the middle of the crosswalk, expecting an answer. A waiting motorist leaned on the horn. A woman pushed a double stroller past, surveying us as I turned to Sean. My hand probably felt like frozen fish bones. His was warm. Rather than answering, I kissed him lightly on the lips, which made his eyes flip fully open like blinds.

He looked surprised, and then he smiled, and we raced across the street holding hands. If someone had shown me that moment on video, I would have said it wasn't me.

I knew then that I would not be going home as planned.

CHAPTER 9

"DUMB"

"You seem far away, little miss," said Gillian.

After leaving Sean, I suddenly felt deflated, as if none of it had happened. I knew I might never see him again, though he had talked about getting together in Victoria. Words were just words.

"Sorry, tired," I said. I was used to getting away with minimal conversation with Verne. It was not so easy with Gillian.

"How's Verne doing?" she asked, her back turned to me as she lifted a bag from the vegetable crisper. She'd already asked me that the night before. Maybe she was trying for a more detailed answer.

"I guess he's okay. It's hard to tell." I scratched at a sticky patch on her kitchen table.

"Sometimes I wonder if Verne is depressed. He's so

quiet and low-key, as if he's having psychomotor retardation." She whacked carrots into medallions with an enormous knife. Gillian was constantly diagnosing people. She usually got that out of her system early in the visit.

"Verne's not retarded," I said, though I knew she meant something else.

"Oh, no. It just means doing things slowly. But then, he's always been that way, methodical. You know, he never got those migraines until after your mother . . ." She trailed off. Verne took pills every day to prevent his blinding headaches. He called the pain "the white wolf," after the white lights he saw before the migraine descended.

"What are we doing tomorrow?" I asked, changing the subject.

"Anything you like. Windy, rainy Seattle is at your feet."

"I'd like to go to some record stores and see the Experience Music Project."

"You've become a serious music fan." There was a pause. She was probably thinking I was like my mother.

"Are you still against bean sprouts, or was that a phase?" she asked, holding up a pack of them.

"Neutral. They used to remind me of worms, but I'm over that."

She turned on the tap to rinse the sprouts. "Did you like my mother?" I asked loudly, to be heard over the water.

"Yes," she said, with only a second of hesitation. "She was lovely, beautiful, always quiet with me. We were close to the same age, but she was really into the music scene and I . . . Different things. We didn't relate, exactly. Maybe she thought I was judging her. But when she was with her friend Janey, different story. With Janey she was bubbly."

"She had me too young," I said. "She wasn't ready."

"Well . . . Annalee adored you. She thought you were amazing. Verne has trouble expressing his feelings."

"Right, family curse. We're incapable of telling the truth." I had heard it before. If I was the light of her life, why did she leave? Then my gregarious, wavy-haired aunt came over and wrapped her muscled arms around me. Sometimes when I felt the sadness crashing over my head, I would recite the facts I knew about Annalee: she liked to hike; she was a Gemini; she was messy but charming; a bee sting could kill her, so she wore a MedicAlert bracelet. I remember it jangling.

"Let's watch a movie, early start, then full-on Seattle," Gillian said.

"Okay."

We watched *The Princess Bride*, which was funny, violent, and romantic all in one. After, I lay in her office and pulled out my Discman. I thought about Cobain again and how two men in his family had killed themselves. He told friends that he had the suicide gene. People later offered that remark as part of the proof that he killed himself, that he hadn't been murdered or faked his death. I think it was just a joke, a sick joke.

I grabbed the CD of *Bleach* to study the lyrics. The drummer on the album was Chad Channing, the guy with silky brown hair who looked like an elf. When I tugged out the liner notes, there was a yellow paper jammed in the CD. I thought it was a receipt at first, but it was a page torn from a lined notepad. *Dear Kurt, By now you're back in Seattle, and I'm still here in sleepy Victoria. After seeing you those two nights, I realized Janey was right. I should have followed the tour. Were you teasing me?*

The page was torn there, the bottom ripped off. It was a note that was never sent. Kurt Cobain was also known to write all kinds of letters and notes, then not mail them. His journals were full of them, I had read. But this note was from my mother. I had read every scrap of paper in the house with her writing on it: old letters, calendars, and a birthday card with an image of Snow White (*Let your heart dream*, the caption read) that she'd given me when I turned three.

My mother had been at the Nirvana show at the Commodore in Vancouver the night before the Victoria concert. She'd taken the passenger ferry across the Strait of Georgia, waited through the ninety-minute crossing so she could see Nirvana, a yet-to-be-famous band, not once, but twice. She'd literally crossed the ocean to see him. Lots of people traveled to see bands, but usually not such an obscure one. Perhaps she'd just been dreaming when she wrote the note, the same way girls scrawl their first names with the last names of boys they like. Something about the band, and him, had captivated her. That was when I thought: What if my mother hadn't just loved Nirvana? What if she'd been in love with Kurt Cobain?

It must have sucked to be Jan Brueghel II. He wasn't as good a painter as his father, not in the same league, and worse, he had eleven kids, which is just excessive. I smiled, imagining what Obe would have said about Jan Brueghel "the Younger." He probably would have concocted other Jans, such as "Jan Brueghel, the Semipro Wrestler" or "Jan Brueghel, the Pastry Chef." Obe would have loved the Experience Music Project Museum, from the crazy Frank Gehry building design to all its sci-fi and horror exhibits, and especially the hip-hop exhibition. I had been expecting music, but not art. There was this exhibition called "DoubleTake: From Monet to Lichtenstein." Gillian listened to me babble about the paintings, happy to see me so animated, so I played it up. I think she felt as if she were watering a plant.

Was I supposed to like Roy Lichtenstein's paintings, which were comics? Sometimes I felt too late for everything. Monet reminded me of Kleenex box designs, but when I saw one close up, it was like climbing into a sunlit lake. I felt calm, a sensation that always darted out of my reach.

"What do you think?" asked Gillian. She wore a deep rose scarf looped around her neck, which brought color to her cheeks. If I asked her about her boyfriends (or girlfriends), would she tell me the truth? Lichtenstein's piece in the show was *The Kiss*, which depicted a serviceman and a blond vixen embracing. It would have been a perfect segue. The Lichtenstein was paired with a painting by Renoir of a woman reading alone, at home in her skin, in peace.

"I like that one," I said, pointing to the Renoir.

"Not the kissing?" She laughed, giving me a look. I would not talk about boys with her. Which meant I had no excuse to ask about her love life.

"No," I said hastily.

Having seen almost everything, we walked out onto the front steps to take one last look at the building.

"Can you imagine leaving something like this behind?" she asked, sweeping her arm across the pewter-gray sky.

"What do you mean?" I asked. Was she asking about suicide? I would not talk about that either.

"I mean the building. The Gehry building. I can't imagine leaving something so amazing behind, as a legacy."

I looked up at it. It *was* amazing. The building fit together, but it looked warped, as if the parts had traveled through another dimension and then were gift wrapped in shiny shades of silver and purple.

"Gillian, you save people's lives. Their lives *are* your legacy."

She shrugged. "I help patch them up a bit. I'm a walk-on character."

"Young lady," I scolded. "You have serious self-esteem issues." I hooked arms with her. "You'll never land a man that way."

Gillian wore the newsboy cap again, as if it were her costume for arrivals and departures. She was invited to come to Victoria for Christmas but had declined. She'd be on duty. She always worked Christmas so the nurses with children could book time off. It was just her way. Gillian did this with no sense of self-pity.

"When are you going to come back and see me again, ducky?" she asked, a tear collecting in the corner of her eye. "I love my drawing, by the way."

She had already told me that three times. I had done a sketch of her, imagining her on the job with a whirl of gurneys and movement, arms and legs, emergencies. I'd called it *Code Blue*, a cheerful holiday sentiment. She seemed to like it, though, the idea that I'd tried to picture her life, and that I had actually been listening to her stories. The sketch was black-and-white, but there was a tornado of blue in one corner meant to be a child in trouble, alone.

Gillian crushed me against her chest again and stroked my hair. We stood in the parking lot of the Clipper terminal as icy rain pelted down, other passengers dashing past us with their rolling suitcases packed with purchases, everyone shopping their brains out for Christmas.

"You sure I can't come in?" she asked.

"I'm fine," I said. She was clearly torn between wanting to see me safely through customs and letting me have the sense that yes, I could do it.

She stepped back and locked the car. "I'll just make sure you get past the guy in the gray uniform."

The lady who took my ticket was not friendly. She

looked me up and down with disdain, her lashes thick with black mascara. I could tell she thought I was a teen runaway, probably pregnant. I pushed back my shoulders. My aunt stood by the doors, her arms folded across her chest, waiting. She always found it hard to see me go, I know. Everyone wanted to help try to fix me.

"Victoria your hometown?" the Clipper clerk asked. I imagined she'd bought all her Christmas gifts at a big box store in the summer to avoid the rush. She wore thick beige foundation so smooth that her cheeks reminded me of panty hose.

"Yes," I said. "I was born there." I knew I looked like shit. I had stayed up thinking, imagining my mother dancing at the Commodore in Vancouver, then rushing back to Victoria to catch the show at the Forge. My brain, and my stomach, had churned all night. When I'd fallen asleep, I'd dreamed of Annalee. She wore a red flower in her hair, and she was smiling, which made me wake up feeling calm.

The Clipper woman rolled her eyes. Why did she hate me so much? I was glad my aunt was standing there. When I turned to her one last time, Gillian waved slowly, as if wiping a mirror. I tried to smile and followed the crowd.

I found a seat in the waiting room but sat closer to the front to score a window on the ferry. I wanted to see this daylight crossing. Let the old people scowl as I upended up their elaborate seating plans. I didn't care anymore.

After landing a window seat, I stretched my feet out in my black Converse with the holes in the toes. I pulled my jacket to my chin and clamped my eyes shut, my ears plugged into my CD player. I must have fallen asleep, because when I opened my eyes, the boat was already plowing across the winter-gray water, the seats filled, clusters of people all holding the same burgundy coffee cups. I searched the scene, looking for someone sketch-worthy. There was a man with a crew cut and leathery red skin who looked like a sailor. He was probably just an accountant who liked the sun. A young couple sat together wearing identical styles of Mountain Equipment Co-op jackets (hers red, his orange), their hiking boots crossed at the ankles the same way. They sipped water from Nalgene bottles with silver carabiners dangling from them. They seemed ready for disaster. There was an old woman, maybe eighty, who wore a carnation-pink dress with a white lace collar. The fabric was a shade normally reserved for baby clothes, but I liked it. It suggested a joy in how she dressed, in life.

An urn of complimentary coffee sat on a minibar by the washrooms. I would have to watch my money. Free was good. My thoughts from the night before had left me exhausted, each one a speeding train. Bending to pick up the creamer I'd dropped, I stood up too quickly. Head rush, then a wave of nicotine. A man was returning from the outside deck, where he had obviously been smoking. I saw his footwear first: brown leather 1964 classic Daytons, biker boots made in East Vancouver. They were originally logging boots, but then bikers and rock stars discovered them. Obe had been raving about them for months. He seemed to covet a pair even more than a girlfriend. The man wore a camel-colored jacket with the hood pulled over his head. He took strangely long strides for a small man. The jacket had funny fasteners on the front that looked like tiny elephant tusks. He wore sunglasses, which was odd since the sun would not return to the Pacific Northwest for weeks. He, too, was alone in a seat of four. We were the only ones on the top deck without company.

The coffee was steaming hot but not strong enough. The man leaned against the ship window, resting his head as if it were heavy, filled with ball bearings. I pulled out my sketchbook, trying to watch him in my peripheral vision. He removed his sunglasses and set them on the table, then took out a sketchbook from his courier bag. When I saw his face, it was like a drawbridge slamming down for me to cross.

I knew: I was sitting across from Kurt Cobain.

I pulled out my pack of pencils, grabbed one, and scrutinized the page. I could not think. I could not draw. My brain had been flash frozen. All around me, families had spread out small feasts of cinnamon buns and cheese bought at Pike Place Market, or sealed tubs of snacks purchased from the Clipper staff. A young woman in the blue-collared uniform was making the rounds, taking orders. I watched her approach the man, who waved her away, averting his eyes.

It seemed I'd been sitting there for hours, not breathing, when he stood up again, heading toward the lavatories. There were two small washrooms, unisex, side by side. I waited until he was locked in one, which reminded me of a cryogenics pod from a movie. I waited, pretending I needed to go next, despite the green vacancy sign lit up on the other one. I put my hand on the wall to steady myself. The earth's tectonic plates seemed to be shifting.

The door burst open, slamming against my hand. I fell back, surprised at the pain, and the man weaved forward to break my fall. As he caught me, his hood fell down and I saw what I had been expecting. The fine nose, the five-o'-clock shadow, but most of all the blazing blue eyes, now wide with alarm. As he grabbed my arms, he said something like *sorry, sorry*. I only heard a white sound, the way you do when you press a conch shell to your ears. The sound is not the ocean. It's your own blood, roaring.

The man held on to my other hand, perhaps afraid I would keel over. He stared at me, mouth half open. Was he too surprised to speak? Or did he see that my eyes were the same shade as his own? We both whispered, not wanting to draw attention. The loud chorus was my heart, which crashed against my chest.

"I'm sorry," he said, turning his face away. "Is your hand okay?"

There was a thick cut like a puckered lip down my knuckle and halfway down the back of my hand, dividing it in two. Blood dripped out. He guided me into the washroom. We could only both fit because he was built like a ruler. Kurt Cobain had not changed.

"Should I call someone over? Your parents? I didn't see you there."

He turned the tap on and I placed my hand under the cold water. The sink was the size of a child's play kitchen. It made us both seem large and clumsy. His wrists were pale and thin, with a branch of soft-blue veins running under the skin.

He stepped back out of the bathroom, as if suddenly aware that he was standing there with a strange teenage girl. I wanted to say it was okay: I knew who he was, but I wouldn't tell. How had he managed it? He'd made some key people believe he was dead, and then the news took off like a flock of pigeons. Not impossible. He was a performer, after all.

"It's all right," I said. "It's just a small cut, on the surface." I felt woozy when I saw my own blood rushing down the drain. I wasn't good with blood. I had my high pain threshold, though. It wasn't my first choice of superpowers, but it could be useful.

He looked relieved and nodded, leaving me to finish washing the cut. I quickly soaped it down with the pink liquid and pressed a brown paper towel against it. I worried he might bolt, disappear somewhere on the ship. I could not lose Cobain. It did not seem right to think of him as Kurt. I had known other Kurts but no other Cobain. In "Serve the Servants" from *In Utero*, Nirvana's final album, Cobain professed to be bored and old, although he was still in his twenties. In his "suicide note" he wrote that the joy had gone from making music. I had never really believed that he killed himself, and now here he was, sailing away from Seattle, the city where he'd owned a large, drafty mansion with his wife.

I returned to my seat, keeping my head down. This was tough, given my blue hair and bleeding hand. I watched him. He was sketching, occasionally glancing my way to see if I was looking. Cobain took out a bag of something, maybe mixed nuts, and scooped up a handful. It seemed a healthy choice for a man who used to survive on hamburgers and Kraft dinner and was staunchly against vegetables. Of course, he would have been thirty-nine, turning forty in February the next year, on the twentieth, to be precise. You couldn't eat like a kid forever. But Cobain had always been thin—skinny, really. Even before he took up with the heroin, or heroine, as he spelled it.

"Would you like to order any drinks or snacks?" The blond server from the Clipper peered down, trying not to stare at the bloody paper towel stuck to my hand.

"Um, no thanks." Gillian had packed me a ziplock bag of snacks, which I had not opened and could not possibly eat. I realized that my thoughts had not latched on to anyone or anything for a few minutes. It was as if I were completely untethered, suspended above the scene on the boat. Was that what heroin was like? Or was it more like riding a fast carousel, or pulling out the motor that makes you feel? Who did you love more, I could ask him: my mother, or heroin? I guess that answer was clear.

It was too soon for all that. I had to watch and wait, two things at which I excelled. So I did a drawing of Cobain as he bent over his sketchbook, his hair falling over his still-beautiful face. He'd exchanged the sunglasses for a pair of thick-rimmed hipster glasses, the kind he wore in the video for "In Bloom." I read that he'd kept the glasses after the shoot and worn them until someone said they made him resemble his father, Donald. Then he'd ditched them.

His hair was still sandy, but it had darkened slightly over the years and fell to his jaw. He could tuck it back and look respectable. Perhaps strangers told him that he kind of looked like an older Kurt Cobain.

I could hardly dare to think it: we held a pencil the same way, Cobain and I.

Cobain had pulled a gray knit cap over his eyes to sleep. He was not traveling with a guitar case, of course. That would have been stupid. But there would be a guitar somewhere, for sure. If Kurt Cobain was alive, he would still be playing a guitar. He would have at least one stashed wherever he was hiding. The guitar would probably be a Fender, and a left-handed one, at that.

I pressed my shoulders against the seat, hard, trying to stop the trembling that ran through my body. I pulled out my cell phone for the first time in two days and dialed, hoping we were close enough for reception. He'd be working until the last minute. *Pick up, pick up, pick up.* He answered.

"It's Nico," I said, annoyed at how girlish I sounded.

"Nico!" His delight at hearing my voice stopped me for

a second, as if I'd just been whacked in the chest by a turnstile. "I've got a tree."

"A real tree?" I asked, despite myself. We hadn't had a Christmas tree since I was six.

"Yes," said Verne, who never used two words when one would do.

"Great," I said. I loved the smell of Christmas trees, even though I hated the holidays. "Listen, the ferry is going to be late. We were delayed in Seattle. We'll be about forty-five minutes behind schedule."

"Okay," he said. "I'll be there earlier, though, just in case."

There was a pause.

"I missed you, Nico."

"Me too," I blurted out. My knuckles were white from clenching the phone. The cut on my hand stung, the paper towel damp with blood.

"Okay." I felt I had to say more. "I saw that restaurant that we went to once, the Chinese one at Pike Place Market. Remember, it had that amazing view of Puget Sound?"

"I do remember," he said. "Gillian took us there when you were nine. You tried hot-and-sour soup."

"That was a good day," I said. My battery was low. I had to get off the phone.

"See you soon, Nico."

I hung up, hoping he wouldn't call the Clipper terminal to check on our arrival, because the sailing, despite the wind, was right on time.

Cobain had opened his eyes and packed up his

sketchbook and was now listening to his headphones. In my limited experience with ferries, the final moments were always tedious: the empty drink cups to be collected, the whiny children, the staff who looked as if they were thinking *Get the fuck off already.*

What was Cobain listening to? Even almost thirteen years after his supposed death, meeting Kurt Cobain would have ensured my popularity for life if I had photographic evidence, or some kind of proof. I could have worn a diaper to school after that and it wouldn't have nullified my status. Sure, your parents might have had Nirvana albums, but Kurt Cobain had left the earth young, like James Dean, when he was still charismatic, despite his hard living. He would never do a television special looking bloated and balding. He would never recite an infomercial, sell out by singing at an oil sheik's wedding, or lend his name to a line of shoes at Walmart. It was better to burn out, and he did, at least on the public record.

Cobain had shunned mainstream popularity on the one hand while rabidly pursuing rock stardom with the other, berating his managers for inadequate promotion, and dumping Seattle's Sub Pop for a bigger label. Cobain was, it seemed, the most ambitious twentysomething slacker you could ever meet.

Cobain had wanted out, obviously, since he faked his death by shotgun, perhaps by dishing out payments to the Seattle police, the coroner's office, and the media. I was still putting the pieces together. I knew it sounded crazy. It *was* crazy.

Based on his past preferences, I figured perhaps his music of choice these days was the Vaselines, Shonen Knife, the Pixies, maybe vintage pop like ABBA or "Seasons in the Sun" by Terry Jacks, a childhood favorite of his that Nirvana once covered. It could be anyone, really, for Cobain had an encyclopedic knowledge of pop and rock; even his detractors agreed on that. And he had detractors. "Seasons in the Sun" was kind of an odd song for Nirvana to cover, since Seattle was not known for its rays. I looked up from my reverie.

Cobain had disappeared. Damn it. The man was slippery.

Canada welcomed me back, reluctantly, after many questions about my travels and purchases while in the U.S. of A. I dashed into the parking lot, panting. No one was waiting for me, which was what I wanted. In the thin winter light, a figure who looked like Cobain was striding away: gray knit cap, black courier bag, and suitcase. I buckled up my backpack, shouldered my smaller knapsack, and ran. Cobain loped along with purpose. I followed at a distance.

His destination was the Greyhound bus terminal. I skulked by the ticket booths, as close as I dared, watching while he purchased a one-way ticket to Duncan, a town up the island in the Cowichan Valley. He then slumped into a hard-backed chair, crossing his Dayton boots at the ankle. I waited a couple of minutes and then bought my own ticket to Duncan. I had no credit card, so I paid cash. Gillian had given me a hundred dollars for my birthday to spend on new clothes.

Once on the bus, I rummaged around in my knapsack until I found two withered fabric bandages and pressed them on my hand. The wound still throbbed, but the bleeding had stopped. I read *Naked Lunch* by William S. Burroughs on the bus ride. Tried to read it, at least. I couldn't concentrate. I was electrified by what I was doing. Cobain didn't seem to notice me the whole two hours. When he stepped off the bus at a sprawling mall, I did, too. I yanked my backpack down from the overhead storage area, clocking some old lady on the head. It seemed I suddenly had no idea how to do anything, as if I were a newborn.

The mall was crazytown, crammed with families reuniting, people fighting for parking spaces. Mostly it was just cars and trucks slowly circling. Cobain kept his head down as he dodged them. I followed. I had expected him to get on another bus, but instead he located a rusty red-and-gray beater in the lot. He tossed his suitcase in the backseat and his satchel in the front and started up the car. This was unexpected. I had thought there would be more buses, or walking, or that he would turn around and recognize me. He jammed a CD in the player and cranked up the volume with a flick of his wrist, higher, higher, until the car was practically vibrating. The car rolled away, pointing toward the exit. Then he stopped and cut the engine, leaving the car parked at the angle of a backslash. Cobain slogged through the parking lot, hands jammed in his pockets. He appeared preoccupied, and I wondered what he could have forgotten. Then I realized he was being drawn to the yellow light of a doughnut shop.

That was my chance. I ran to the car, clicked open the back door, wedged my packs onto the dirty floor mats, and then flopped myself down. There was a red-and-green-plaid blanket draped over the seat, so I pulled that over myself, the wool fringe tickling my nose. I heard him slam the door, swear at his plastic coffee lid, and crinkle some wax paper.

He was trying to leave the lot at the same time as a bunch of other vehicles, either manic Christmas shoppers or drivers who had just claimed their relatives at the bus depot.

"Fuckety fuckety fuck fuck," Cobain pronounced. I willed my whole body, even my lungs, to be still. Then he started up the stereo again. I was in. Free of the parking lot, he peeled away while the car shook with the Pixies. The album was *Surfer Rosa*, oh my golly.

CHAPTER 10

"NEGATIVE CREEP"

After what seemed like hours, Cobain killed the engine, and there was three-ply silence for a moment. Then I heard a sound like a bird strangling as he yanked the parking brake. We had arrived somewhere. I had never known it was possible for a whole body to shake, but mine did as he slammed the car door, boots scraping on dirt. I'd always pictured him wearing Converse, as he did in the old days. But he would not want to be recognized; hence the Daytons. Every day thousands of people posted blogs about him, commented on online videos; there was talk of musicals, new documentaries, and on and on. It's not as if anyone ever really let him be dead.

I heard another door clack open. My stomach rocked to one side.

"Holy shit!"

A pause. Cold air blasted in. The smell of pine or fir, something green. Wind bashed the trees, an ominous supernatural howling. There would be a storm for Christmas.

"What the fuck is *this*?"

"I can explain." My voice disappeared into the plastic floor mat. I was lying on my packs, facedown. I had to shimmy myself along to get my feet out the car door so I could stand and look at Cobain. My hair fanned up, probably looking like a blue toilet brush. Cobain's mouth hung open. He raised his hand to try to run it over his hair, forgetting he was wearing a hat.

I had no idea where we were except that it was somewhere in the woods, somewhere near Duncan. The car was parked on a patch of gravel surrounded by towering trees, which were shaking like crazy in the storm. I almost wished I were back home with Verne and his Christmas tree.

"Who sent you?" he demanded, slapping his thin arms around himself in a gesture almost violent in its suddenness.

"What? No one. My name is Nico. I think you once met my mother." I had a knot in my chest where I'd been lying on the packs.

"Tell me why you were in my car before I call the police," he said, taking a step back as if my mental disorder were contagious.

I dissected his syntax, a surprising calm enveloping me. Did he mean I had to tell him or he'd call the police, or that he needed to give the police my reason? It was unclear. But

Cobain wouldn't really call the police. He had too much to hide, possibly more than I was guessing.

"I know that you knew my mother," I said, almost shouting to be heard above the wind. At that moment his hat flew off and he chased it, pushed into action again, his shock interrupted.

I lifted my packs out and shouldered them, prepared to follow. My legs wobbled under me. When had I last eaten? The rain started up, the kind that feels like thumbtacks firing down. Then I heard a roaring in my ears and I keeled over, as if I were a five-foot-five-inch sandbag. Someone snuffed out the lights, and that was it. When I regained consciousness, Cobain was carrying me somewhere along a gravel path. The rain pelted from above and fingers of wind tugged at my hair. I had forgotten where I was until I saw Cobain hefting me along, his blond hair flopping over his cheek. The grim look on his face, fixated and fierce, scared me. I told my body to move, but I hung there, limp.

"Sorry," I mumbled. "What happened?"

"You passed out," he said, still half carrying me, his arm slung under my rib cage. "A bad storm coming in. I have to get rid of you."

"Huh," I said, wondering where I had left the food Gillian packed me. What time was it anyway? Was it Christmas?

We approached a log cabin. Cobain unlocked the door. It took a long time, as if there were multiple locks, which seemed excessive in the woods. There was the smell of woodsmoke and something else, maybe Scotch, which Verne drank once or twice a year. "This where you live?" I asked in a raspy whisper. Cobain dumped me on a lumpy bed with a thick patchwork quilt. My brain was churning. All the signs pointed to danger. I didn't know what to think, but I wanted to see it through, no matter what happened.

"I'll get you some food," said Cobain. "Then we can talk. And then you can leave."

Stone-faced, he brought me squares of processed cheddar cheese and round Ritz crackers. Processed food. I almost smiled.

"Do you have any strawberry Quik?" I asked. A test. I grabbed a cracker and cheese, chewing like a rabid squirrel.

"What? No," he said, impatient. "Listen, I seem calm, but I am fucking freaking out, so talk. What are you doing here? Did Shelley send you?"

The cabin was what realtors call open concept, where the living room and bedroom blend together. There was the single bed I sat on, a burgundy leather couch patched with duct tape, a woodstove, a woven rug, and a coffee table. Next to the door was a galley kitchen, cheap green tile on the floor. By the bed sat one brown fake-wood kitchen table and two chairs, the plastic-covered kind you can wipe down with a cloth.

"Fuck's sake! Start talking." That voice. It was still boyish, with a bored overtone despite the surface panic. I could close my eyes and imagine him saying "This was written by the *Va-se-lines*."

"I wanted to meet you," I said. The food fired up my brain again, a gray cement mixer churning to life.

"Why?" he asked, his blue eyes fixed on me as if trying to decide whether that made my being a stowaway better or worse.

"Who's Shelley?" I asked. I hadn't even thought about there being another woman involved, a new girlfriend, or even—a wife? Cobain was on the lam, a fugitive from his old life. Surely he was alone, like me. We seemed so much the same. It was clear: Kurt Cobain was alive, and I had found him. I had found my real father.

"I'll ask the questions," he said. "Who do you belong to, and how do I reach them?" He paced around the cabin in sock feet. He wore thick hiking socks, sensible. Cobain used to wear layer upon layer of clothes, including long underwear, because he was so sensitive about his slight build. Layers were wise. The wind screeched through the trees. No one on the planet knew where I was.

"Does this place have its own generator?" I asked.

"Cops. Calling," he said, pointing to a cell phone that we both knew wouldn't work. We were in the boonies of Vancouver Island during a windstorm. "I'm going to drive you back to the bus station. This is bullshit."

"I think you knew my mother. Her name was Annalee Lester back then."

"Can I call her right now?"

"She's gone. No one knows where she is. She disappeared."

"That's what this is about? You think I know where she is?" He sat down on one of the kitchen chairs, keeping a good distance between us. There was a guitar case at his feet under the kitchen table. He'd have more guitars somewhere. I noticed a funny little door by the kitchen, perhaps once a pantry. What did it hold? Not drugs, I hoped. The way he was using when he staged his exit, it was clean up or die. He must have chosen to kick the drugs in private, in peace.

"No, I don't think anything," I said, lying. "Where are we, anyway?"

"What's with the blue hair?" he asked, probably trying to catch me off guard. Cobain was no stranger to the Kool-Aid dye job. "You aren't exactly the cheerleader type, are you."

The last line was delivered in a dry sneer. I knew Cobain could be cruel, unless you were a child or an animal. I was neither. I was a major inconvenience.

"There are no cheerleaders at Vic High," I said, and then winced at my stupidity.

"Right. We're going back to the bus station, and I'll send you on your way back to Victoria." He smiled, as if pleased that he had outwitted me so quickly. He rubbed the scruff on his chin. Even as a middle-aged man, he wasn't interested in a clean shave.

What I really wanted was for him to sing, just for me, preferably "All Apologies." Then I wanted him to tell me everything he remembered about that night in 1991, and my mother, and her dancing, and her hair, and her laugh. Granted, it had been almost sixteen years, but Cobain didn't seem that old. He still looked good, despite the scruff, the messy hair, and the years of hard living. It was a bizarre thing to think about your own father, but it was true. If my real father was so beautiful, perhaps one day I could be, too? I did have his eyes.

"Nico, or whatever your name is, I'm done playing." He rose from the chair and grabbed my forearm, hard. "I can't have anyone find you here, so you've got to leave now."

"Storm's too bad," I gasped, alarmed at his grip. I could feel each finger pressing in. When you played guitar as much as Cobain did, it gave you strong fingers but took a toll. Carrying the instrument made his back worse, which made his stomach pain worse, which contributed to his heroin use, or so he said. I would have to ask him if he really had scoliosis. The various biographies had left me confused.

We faced each other.

"There will be power lines down, guaranteed." I figured we were somewhere near Nanaimo, maybe Cedar or Cassidy, one of those small rural patches. I couldn't tell how far we'd driven. Cobain relaxed his grip.

"You cannot be here," he said, each word as sharp as a karate kick. "I don't know what you want, but I'm telling you to get up and walk to the door. I'll drive you to the bus station. Move it, or things could get nasty."

"I know who you are."

That stopped him. The fury fell from his face like a coat slipping off a hook.

"Oh, you do. Who am I?"

"You're my father," I said, expecting to feel relief or perhaps terror. I waited, mostly feeling nothing but a vague need to pee.

"Kid," Cobain sighed, his adrenaline fading. "You've got problems. And a massive imagination." He took two steps back from me, causing the floorboards to creak. A branch smacked one of the cabin windows, making a thud like a bird.

"I will carry you out of here if I have to."

It seemed he meant it. I was going to need more time. I had waited too long and come too far. Perhaps I had always been that crazy, and Obe and Verne had kept me on an even keel, following the rules.

"If you carry me out of here, I will report you at the bus station and say you kidnapped me." My brain spun. "Don't you think all those people on the Clipper heard the commotion in the bathroom? I'll say you were trying to grab me." I thrust my bandaged hand into the air.

"You must be my punishment," he said, spitting.

"Would anyone really believe I crawled into the backseat of your car?" I didn't ask him why he was being punished. It could be anything. There was no rhyme or reason for punishment. "I just want to talk to you," I said. "Then I'll go."

Cobain sat back down, still wearing his coat, as if unsure he wanted to stay in his own cabin. He threw off his hat and raked his fingers through his hair. The cabin was freezing. I could probably figure out the woodstove if he left. I had been a latchkey kid for years. I liked to think I had inner resources.

"I have work to do," he snapped, sinking his forehead into one hand. "You're not going to be my problem anymore."

That was when I noticed the photographs along the wall. Of bodies, or rather body parts, cut into sections.

CHAPTER 11

"SERVE THE SERVANTS"

Cobain's core seemed to be made of something unsubstantial, as if he were a balsa model airplane. His posture was even worse than mine.

"What's your name?" I began. A test.

"Daniel," he said.

"Daniel what?" He had possibly taken the name from Daniel Johnston, the artist and singer. Cobain had worn a T-shirt featuring one of Johnston's cartoons to the 1992 MTV music awards. If Cobain wore your shirt, it could *make* you. If I walked through Vic High with him, heads would turn. Sure, not everyone my age would recognize him right away, but Cobain gave off an "I don't give a fuck" vibe that would be irresistible.

"Daniel Boone," said Cobain. "Hence the cabin."

"If you're not going to tell me the truth, say 'pass.' I've had enough people lie to me."

"Pass. You can just call me Daniel," said Cobain, shoving kindling into the stove. He was awkward at it, fumbling. It was like watching a puppet chef trying to stuff a turkey. "A better question is who do you think I am?"

I kept sneaking looks at the body parts lined up along the wall. Cobain had always done art, and it was out there; in fact, some biographers said he was obsessed with images of diseased vaginas and bodily functions in general. The man also owned collections of toy monkeys and dolls, which he broke and used in his art. It all made sense.

Unless I was wrong.

What if Cobain had gone truly insane? A dime-sized corner of my brain wondered: what if this guy wasn't Cobain? Some psychopaths acted on opportunity, I had read. And this would be the perfect opportunity. The stove door slammed shut, and I jumped. I would not fare well heading out on foot. My clothes were too thin against the winter storm raging outside. I needed layers: lined boots, fleece, Gore-Tex, and goose down.

The kitchen had a shiny toaster, an ancient Mr. Coffee with white daisies printed on the pot, and a wood block containing black-handled knives. I backed toward the counter. Could I grab a knife without him noticing? Cobain/Daniel was still crouched by the stove, facing the glass door. Would a knife even do any good? It was getting dark, four-thirty on Christmas Eve, and I had no idea where I was. Those body parts in the pictures had once belonged to real people. Girls, perhaps. What kind of person hid out in the woods? One with something to hide. He could be crazy and Cobain, or crazy and not Cobain. No, no, he had to be Cobain.

"Well, I can't have you faint again," he said, whapping some fireplace ash from his hands. "You want Kraft mac and cheese?"

I laughed, a bark of relief. Of course he would have a box of macaroni. Cobain existed on it.

"Yeah," I said. "I'm still starving." I sat down at the kitchen table. The plastic seat was cold. I traced the whorls in the fake wood. "Do you want me to make it?"

"No. Let me do it," he said, in a telephone-operator tone. Cobain had a few wrinkles around his eyes, but he still had the voice of a young man. Some said he had one of the best voices in rock ever, not for power or purity, but meaning that he knew how to put a song across, to transmit it. His voice could be harsh, or growling, or soft and sweet, or he could scream like a wounded crow.

Cobain brought the pot right to the table, along with two forks and two mismatched cereal bowls. Let the record show that Cobain made an exemplary pot of bright orange macaroni, and we ate together in wary silence.

Afterward, he set the pot in the sink to soak. (Cobain would never be a dish doer.) "How about you tell me why you're here. There must be people worried about you. And shit, the authorities. It would be a—what is it?"

"Amber Alert. It's when kids get kidnapped." I really needed to pee, but I had a feeling Cobain's bathroom might be horrifying. "Interesting pictures you have."

"Yeah. It's for my work. I do medical illustrations, free-lance."

That seemed unlikely. He was lying, but I went along with it. I didn't want to make him angrier. He had a temper.

"I'm an artist, too," I said, and felt a knot tighten in my gut. I had never called myself that, not out loud.

"Yeah? Who are your influences?"

Was he making fun of me, the fifteen-year-old who thought she was something? I really thought I was nothing most of the time. I couldn't tell Cobain all that, although I thought he would understand. When Cobain was thirteen, he and a friend saw a body hanging from a tree, a suicide. I had never seen anything so terrible, except when I closed my eyes and pictured what might have happened to my mother.

"Modern," I said. "I guess I like modern. Simple lines, abstract, and sometimes a little crazy." I did not have the words for all the art terms. Or if I did, they escaped me.

"Crazy is okay," he said softly. Then he shook both fists in the air like a preacher. "CRAZY IS O-KAY!" he yelled, his eyes bugging. Then he dropped his hands. "What kind of music do you like?" he asked, as if the outburst hadn't occurred. Cobain could talk about music—or play it—for hours on end. I swung back to feeling sure, again, that this man was really Cobain. I wondered if he had ever brought his daughter, Frances Bean, to visit the cabin. It appeared not. The place only had the basics, yet still managed to be messy: a den for a lone man to hibernate in.

"Nirvana," I said, staring at him. "I love Nirvana."

"They were pretty good," he agreed. "I was once a big fan. They've been gone a long time, though." His right eye twitched.

"What about you? What do you listen to now?" The cabin was heating up, the wood snapping like Christmas crackers as it burned.

"Swing music," he said. "I like a big horn section."

"No lying," I insisted.

"Yeah, okay, I like the Pixies, you heard that. Listen, I'm getting pissed off. Do you know what they do to men who are caught with young girls? You're going to tell them the truth, right?"

Cobain was fish-belly white at the thought of the authorities. He'd come a long way from the guy who had a sticker on his guitar case that read *Vandalism: As beautiful as a rock in a cop's face.* As a teen he had once tagged the very YMCA where he worked and later been paid to clean up the graffiti. Cobain couldn't lose his nerve. It was too much. I leaned over and slapped him in the face. He needed to help me. He needed to tell the truth.

"What the fuck?" he said, grabbing my wrist.

"You can't lie to me," I said, shaking out my hand. I had never hit anyone before. I was tired of nodding and understanding. Maybe 2007 would be my hitting year.

"Okay. Fuck. Just out with it."

"I think you knew my mother, Annalee. She disappeared when I was four."

"I don't recall ever meeting an Annalee." Cobain rubbed his jaw where I'd landed my slap, which was far from powerful. It had surprised him, though. "But I'm not from here."

"Where are you from?"

"A little town in Washington State. I travel back and forth. I go to see my daughter, when I'm allowed."

I assumed he was talking about Frances Bean, but maybe he'd later had another daughter as well. I badly wanted to tell him that I knew. I pictured him embracing me, awkwardly at first, but then being relieved to have someone know him, really know him. After the shock passed, he would be happy to have another daughter. Perhaps I could even meet Frances Bean, and I would have a half sister.

Cobain moved to sit on the floor by the couch, his feet stretched out by the fire. I joined him, without asking, sitting a foot away so he wouldn't freak out. "There's a song, right? By the Band. 'The Weight.' It has a line about young Anna Lee, and keeping her company," he said, a gesture.

"Yes, of course." Anyone who loved music knew that song. It was almost impossible to listen to it and not feel wistful. A body would be easier, I sometimes thought. A body found and a story. Easier than this long collapse. After eleven years, no news was not good news. Other days, I decided Annalee simply didn't want to be found, and she was on a tropical island sleeping in a hammock and waiting on tables, something she'd done as a teen. I pictured her surrounded by explosions of lush azaleas. She would no longer be a young woman. I thought for a second that I had sobbed out loud, but it was just a gale outside racing through the trees.

"I have a photo of her," I said, grabbing my knapsack. It was the Polaroid, the one taken in Victoria at the Forge.

Cobain took the photo, lifted it up to the firelight. He held it so close that for one awful instant I thought he might throw it in the flames. The cabin had that feeling: anything could happen.

"She was a beauty," said Cobain. "She really was, Nico." He moved to give the photo back to me, then changed his mind and raised it to his face again. "I wish I had known her."

He couldn't get a better look because at that moment the lights went out. There was pure, velvet darkness; then I heard Cobain bumbling around. He lit a hurricane lamp. Whoever owned the cabin had laid in an array of flashlights and lamps. It was likely not Cobain. He did not seem the type to own land, his Seattle mansion days long gone. His face in the half-light made me think of all those grainy online videos of him playing guitar. Sometimes he wore a dress, or even women's lingerie. That was Cobain. Still, he was deeply sensitive and prone to nursing hurts, or so I had read. That was Cobain, too. Yes, he was older, but his face was still boyish, with that dimple in his chin.

"Are you frightened?" he asked. "Because you should be."

"Why?"

"You're in a cabin, during a storm, with some strange

man on Christmas Eve. You should be terrified. What's wrong with you? If my daughter did this, I would kill her."

Cobain's interrogation was beginning to remind me of all the therapists and guidance counselors pressing me to choose a capital-C Career. They didn't understand that if I couldn't have my mother, the only other thing I wanted was to listen to music with Obe and maybe go to art school. If I lasted that long. Sometimes that seemed in doubt. I had thought about *ways*. None of them seemed satisfactory. Some days I simply could not believe in happy endings, or that good things happen to good people, or that everything happens for a reason.

"I'm not afraid," I said, lying. *You have nothing to lose*, I told myself. *Finish this.*

"Your father must be frantic."

"No." The stove crackled. I noticed a hole in the heel of my skate socks, wide, like a gaping mouth. "Can you play me something on the guitar?" I nodded toward the case under the kitchen table. "If you do, I promise I'll go."

Any time the talk turned to music, his mood seemed to improve. He glanced at the guitar, as if it were a parcel he'd forgotten to open.

"I haven't played that in ages. I got it in high school to impress the girls. That's how I got myself a wife. Let that be a lesson," he said, and left it at that.

He crawled on his hands and knees and found the guitar. The darkness seemed thick, pressing down like humidity. My hair would smell of woodsmoke. I heard something skitter across the floor and it occurred to me that we were not alone in the cabin. There were creatures with tails.

Cobain opened the case and in the dim light strummed the opening chords to AC/DC's "Back in Black."

"That's the first song you learned to play," I said.

"No, it was 'Stairway to Heaven.' It must have been 'Stairway.'"

"You liked the Beatles and the Monkees."

"Sure, everyone did. Look, what's wrong with you? I mean, what's the matter?"

"I guess I'm just too much of a moody baby," I said, my final lob over the net, quoting from his supposed suicide note. I heard crying: gasping chain-saw sobs. It was coming from me.

"Hey," he said, putting his arm around me. I wiped my nose with the back of my hand and rested my cheek against his sleeve. He wore a flannel shirt, of course, soft from years of wear. Cobain's hand hung over my chest like a starfish. I was so tired. Outside, branches smacked against the window.

"Help me, Cobain," I thought, and must have whispered out loud.

"What did you call me?" he asked.

"I need to use your bathroom." I couldn't put it off any longer. He handed me a flashlight and pointed to the ratty plywood door in the corner of the room. I shined the beam at the door, right on a bashed-in circle, dead center, no doubt made by a fist. From what I could see, the bathroom had a warped floor, a stall with a rusted showerhead and a torn peach curtain. There was a sad toilet with a wooden seat that was cold on my thighs. I peed for what seemed like ten minutes, trying not to touch the seat, while gazing at a large plastic box by the sink. I heard something moving. Oh God, if they were baby rats, I would freak: their pink hooded eyes and soft gray bodies. We'd found a nest of them once at our house in Victoria under the hot water heater. I could handle many things. Rats weren't one of them.

I set the flashlight by the sink, determined to wash my hands. I unstuck a triangle of glycerin soap from the counter. The water sputtered and spat. I dried my hands on my jeans, then pushed the lid off and shined the light in the box. It was alive with bodies. I looked closer. They were baby turtles, four of them, clambering around in a mix of soil and leaves.

"Are you keeping something alive in there?" I asked Cobain. He was sitting up on the couch, still holding the guitar, strumming. He had a small battery-powered lamp going, which cast a watery lemon light.

"Yeah, American box turtles. I'm going to build them a pool in the spring. They like the humidity in the bathroom. They're fan-fucking-amazing," he said, pointing one finger in the air for emphasis.

That was the longest answer I had heard from Cobain. He still kept turtles.

"So," Cobain asked. "Where would I have met your mother?" He had picked up the photo again.

"A club in Victoria, the Forge. March 1991. Nirvana with an AC/DC cover band."

"Oh, yeah," he said, rubbing his chin. "We danced together."

"You pulled her onstage," I corrected him.

"Right, I did, because she was so beautiful, Annalee. She was with a friend. . . ." I could tell by his tone that he was shitting me, playing along to see what I'd say. He was trying to trip me up again.

"Janey. Her best friend: Janey Keogh. They did everything together." It annoyed me that he wasn't even trying to remember. Yes, it was a long time ago and he'd done a lot of drugs in the years after, but he could at least make an effort.

"What happened to Janey?"

He rubbed the bottom of the Polaroid with his thumb as if there might be a hidden message on it. His finger pads were calloused. He played guitar more than he'd admitted.

"When my . . . After Verne and my mother got married, Janey was working at a resort in Whistler. I guess she was a wild one, snowboarding, partying, and all that. Janey was . . . rough."

"Then what?"

"Then what, *what*?"

"What happened to Janey?"

"I guess she was crushed when my mom disappeared. She left the country for Puerto Rico or something. She was the crazy one. Annalee was sensible, most of the time. Or so I'm told."

"Write Janey's full name down on this paper," he said, shoving an Esso gas receipt at me. "Make sure you spell it properly. So Verne, your father, was all you had?"

"I had my aunt. She's why I was in Seattle. A grandmother. That's about it."

I thought I heard the skittering again. My eyes itched from the woodsmoke. It was late.

"Nico," said Cobain. "It's almost Christmas."

"Yeah? I'd better get to sleep or Santa won't come," I said. When had I started talking like that? After I started listening to Nirvana.

"I'm going to give you a present," he said in his soft, boyish voice, easing the guitar back in the case by the light of the fire.

"What's that?" Goose bumps climbed a ladder up my arms. I wasn't used to people just giving me things.

"I'm going to help you find Janey. Tomorrow." He snapped the case shut.

CHAPTER 12

"BREED"

When I was little, in kindergarten, I would sometimes wake up and expect my mother to be standing over my bed. She used to do that. Verne said she liked to watch me sleep, which sounds boring, I know. She would watch my breath rise and fall, my eyes shut tight like a doll's. Some days, I would forget that she was gone, dead, disappeared, and there would be this crackle of joy in me at the thought of seeing her. Then I would remember, and I would cry, howling, until Grandma Irene, who lived with us for a few months, made me wash my face and eat a bowl of cereal. Over the months, I stopped howling and became the Quiet Girl, a walk-on part in a movie.

When I woke up in the cabin, the lights were on, which meant the power had returned. My bones ached because I had been cold, even under the quilt and the blankets.

Cobain had grunted that I should take the bed. He would sleep on the couch. I was only to stay one night, he said several times. I had fallen asleep at once, the quiet like a lake engulfing me. The deep sleep was almost unsettling. At home, I often lay awake. I'd try not to think about having to go to school the next day or my terrors of the Frog Man, this nasty half man, half frog who was the star of my nightmares. If the Frog Man touched you, he would leave warts on your skin. You would never be the same. Verne used to check under my bed for the Frog Man and then leave the light on without me having to ask.

As I peered around, I realized Cobain was gone. He wasn't just in the woodshed, or feeding the turtles, or outside checking the weather. He was gone.

So there it was, Christmas Day, and I was on my own. People had to be searching for me. Verne would want me back, yearning to retrieve me as if I were a lost bicycle. No, Verne did love me. He did. But he didn't fully claim me and make me feel as if I belonged. There was something in him that prevented it. And now it all made sense.

Having nothing else to do, I sketched Cobain playing his guitar. I used my style, spidery arms and legs, motion. I liked Daphne Odjig, a native artist from Ontario. I had seen her prints on cards.

When I was done with the sketch, I tried my cell phone. Verne would be looking for me at the ferry terminal, then everywhere, which made me sad. I could call home and say I was fine but not coming back for a while. But wherever we were was remote enough that we weren't getting reception. The floor creaked as I walked to the fridge and yanked it open. The air smelled of woodsmoke and something else, gasoline and lemon, like an industrial floor cleaner. The cabin had been cleaned at some point. I couldn't imagine Cobain with a mop, though he'd once been a janitor after he dropped out of high school. Like I said, Cobain was an ambitious slacker. He later included a janitor in the "Smells Like Teen Spirit" video as a private joke.

The fridge contained a carton of milk, a jar of raspberry jam, a tub of I Can't Believe It's Not Butter, and four bottles of Rolling Rock. Finding half a bag of English muffins in one of the cupboards, I examined them for mold, then toasted one and ate it. I opened the cabin door and a gust of cold air rushed in. There was a layer of frost on the ground. I glanced at my watch: 8:23 a.m. There were tire tracks in the mud that had been covered over with frost. He would return for his turtles, if not for me, I figured.

Back inside, I decided to snoop. In the cutlery drawer, I found a pack of Winston Lights and an orange Bic lighter. I had hoped for a wallet or passport, but he had taken those with him. Cobain was cagey. I hoped he was off drugs. He'd be able to find those in Nanaimo, no problem. It was a harbor city.

I studied the images of body parts once more, including a photo of the heart: the atria, valves, and ventricles, the arteries springing out like garden hoses. In a small drawer in the coffee table, I found a little illustrated children's book on caring for turtles. American box turtles have a hinge on their lower shell that allows them to retract inside, leaving no flesh exposed. That was something to be envied. There was a laptop on the end table by the bed, but it was password protected, so that was that.

People say "Maybe this Christmas," or "the magic of Christmas," or "I'm dreaming of a white Christmas." I thought this: I could not take one more. I had been waiting for something, someone, to help me, and no one had. I was done. A yellow school bus soars off an icy road; divers search a lake for bodies; legs are crushed; a brain is dead. Sometimes the worst has happened. Sometimes done is done.

I had itemized the ways. For example, Verne took tiny blue pills every day to stave off his headaches. He brought them home from the pharmacy in big quantities because it was cheap. Those would work. There were bridges, such as the blue one downtown on Johnson Street. There were hard drugs that could be purchased at Vic High. And who could blame me surrendering my brain? Perhaps people would be surprised I'd waited so long. Sure, I knew other kids who only had one parent at home, lots of them, but no one else had a mother who had just vanished one day without explanation or warning. Not knowing was killing me in a way that felt literal, a clawing in my gut.

A car door slammed. Cobain was back. I walked outside to check. He was wearing the same hooded coat but with a burgundy hunting-style cap on his head, which was odd, since it screamed Kurt Cobain. The trees were laced with snow, but the wind had died down. It would be a peaceful Christmas—for some.

No doubt Aunt Gillian would be frantic, Verne would be worried, and Grandma Irene would be sure I was dead in a ditch. She was a worst-case-scenario person. And that was about it. Obe would still be in Winnipeg visiting his grandparents, wondering why I hadn't been emailing—unless someone called him looking for me.

Obe, I imagined writing. *I have found my father. I have found Kurt Cobain.* I knew it sounded insane. I needed more time and more proof. I needed Cobain to like me, to love me, to see our connection. I was eager to show him the sketch.

Some people walk. Cobain kind of swooped. I wondered if he still had back problems.

"Nico!" Cobain had a big smile on his face and a coffee in each hand. "This is for you," he said, presenting a red paper cup. "Merry Christmas. It's a latte."

Cobain was acting strange. Jovial. And he had called me by name.

"The end is in sight, Nico, but I have one more thing for you. Come inside."

He opened the cabin door, taking a sip of his coffee.

"You know, I don't like rich people, but I do like their fancy-pants coffee," he said. "I'll admit that to you, and only you."

He sat at the kitchen table and thumped his coffee down. In daylight, I could see that the table needed scrubbing. He dropped the hunting cap on the floor, his hat rack of choice.

"Nico, I think I found Janey."

I said nothing. I clutched the coffee cup, which made my fingertips pulse. The coffee was scalding.

"Did you hear me?"

I nodded. There had been too many close calls, too many disappointments. None of them had ever put me any closer to my mother's arms. Once, there was a serial killer from Spokane, Washington. He was serving a life sentence for murdering several women, including some seasonal farm workers in the Lower Mainland, not far from Vancouver. While doing time, he'd admitted to committing more murders in Canada. For a few months, the police had investigated the possibility that my mother had encountered him, but there was never a strong link.

Annalee Cavan had left Vancouver Island; that was known. There was security-video footage of her taken on the ferry from Swartz Bay to the Tsawwassen terminal on the mainland. I knew, too, from Aunt Gillian that a lot of disturbing questions had been asked about my mother. Sex-trade workers were disappearing from Vancouver's downtown eastside. Poor and drug-addicted women were going missing, and later, bodies were discovered at a farm in the Lower Mainland. But Annalee's DNA was never found, nor was she ever spotted on the streets of Vancouver. Annalee had no history of hard drug use or mental health problems. She had just walked away from her life.

In Vancouver, the trail had gone cold. The last sighting of her was on the *Spirit of Vancouver Island*, a ship that sounds like a ghost but is really a massive ferry that can hold more than four hundred vehicles. She traveled on foot, though, since she had never learned to drive. The ferry could move more than two thousand people. It was an easy place to disappear.

"Nico. This is good news. Or at least news."

I wondered if he'd pounded back a couple of coffees before returning. He was jittery. He picked up the cap again.

"Janey Keogh waitressed at the Blue Peacock Pub in Whistler until the summer of 1996. After that, it looked as if she left to work in Puerto Rico for a few years."

"A few years? You mean she came back?"

"She's in Vancouver. She works at a college day care. I got her home address. It's North Vancouver."

"How do you know all this? About Janey?"

Cobain shrugged. "I know a guy in Nanaimo. He can find out things, for a price. You can get almost anything in Nanaimo for the right price."

"You have a hacker who works on Christmas Day?"

"He did this time. It's just a matter of accessing electronic records. I'll send you the bill."

"You aren't really a medical illustrator, are you?"

"Hmm. Did you do this drawing?" He picked up the sketch.

The answer was obvious, given the circumstances. He was dodging me.

"This is not bad. It's me, right?"

"Yes. It's you. Merry Christmas."

My gift clearly made him uncomfortable, and he fiddled with the strap of the hunting cap.

"I have to feed the turtles," he said, shuffling off but still talking. "They belong to my daughter. Her mother travels a lot, so . . . It's a long story. They trust me with the turtles, at least." He dropped something metal on the floor, cursed, and retrieved it. I could hear him murmuring something to the turtles.

"After that, can you do me one more favor?" I shouted. It was now or never.

$$\mathscr{N}$$

Cobain refused to go with me. We made an agreement: he would drive me to Duke Point. He would not report me, but he would not accompany me on the ferry to Vancouver.

"How can you even ask that? I can't get charged with kidnapping. I was on my own when I was not much older than you, so do what you have to. But at least send word home. Tell them that you're alive."

"Fine," I said, although I thought that was a bit much coming from him. He'd had more than a decade to "send word home."

"And whatever you do, do not mention me."

"I'll send the message right now, before we go. I promise." If the Internet in the cabin was working, which was not a given.

Cobain, from the many stories I had read, was inclined to self-preservation. He feared conflict. He skipped out on people instead of confronting them. Nirvana constantly changed drummers in the early days, but Cobain never fired them face to face.

I didn't want to leave Cobain. Maybe he would go back

to Seattle, or who knew where. I considered presenting all the facts that suggested I was his daughter. But then, he had one daughter already, and he wasn't with her.

I typed: *Verne, delayed. Had to take another trip. Something came up. I am fine. Will see you very soon. XOXO Nico.*

After sending my message and packing up, I made the entire journey to the Duke Point terminal crouched in the backseat, as per Cobain's orders. I didn't dare ask for directions back to the cabin. I was afraid he'd tell me not to come back, so I just kept sticking my head up to look for landmarks—a farmer's market sign, a truck for sale by the side of the road. I caught a glimpse of a street sign before Cobain yelled at me to stay down.

We arrived at 9:45 a.m., enough time to board the 10:15 to Tsawwassen terminal in Vancouver. The authorities would no doubt be checking ferry terminals for me, but likely the main one from Victoria, which was Swartz Bay. I figured I might get lucky. Duke Point was smaller and less busy.

Cobain, too, knew the police would be looking for me. The cops seemed to be a constant preoccupation, and he mentioned them several times. He stopped the car with a lurch to let me out just shy of the terminal. He was only willing to go so far. He was either getting more cautious or smarter with age.

"Couldn't you just go home and then travel to Vancouver with your dad later?" he asked while his car idled. I could see now it was an old Pontiac Phoenix with British Columbia plates.

"I'm not going back there. If I do, I'll never be allowed to leave the house, that's for sure." Verne was not unkind, but he believed in maintaining order and safety. That was his job, at work and at home. I remembered then that he had gotten a tree. The thought of it sitting there undecorated made me sad, but not sad enough to turn around. I hopped out, trying not to seem scared. Forward march.

Passing the statue of an enormous orca that stands by the terminal, I thought that maybe Cobain and I could pose by it together, the big fake whale. It could be ironic, as everything was. I had forgotten about the point-and-shoot camera in my backpack, which hopefully contained at least one good photo of Sean. I turned to wave to Cobain, but he was gone. I'd said I'd only go to Vancouver without him if he promised to be in the cabin when I returned. He did, though he might have had his fingers crossed.

As I approached the kiosk, I realized Verne would have called Gillian, and the workers might be looking for a girl with Kool-Aid blue hair. I pulled my hat on, just in case.

For the first half hour of the ferry ride, I flinched at every footstep, waiting to feel a hand clamp on my shoulder and to be led off to wherever they haul teen runaways. I plugged in my laptop at one of those workstations with little dividers to prevent snooping.

I had the idea of getting myself a Nanaimo bar, because it was Christmas, and when in Rome. I fixated on the idea:

the coconut, the custard, the chocolate. There were few other passengers, so I left my laptop on my seat with my jacket draped on top. When I returned, I ate the square in two bites, sprinkling coconut over the keyboard. I had downloaded fourteen email messages. They all said the same thing: WHERE ARE YOU?

After my mother disappeared, there was silence, phone calls, and silence. When Kurt Cobain disappeared, the world went biblical: candlelit vigils and suicides. Grunge was officially dead, or so everyone said. There's even a photo of Kurt Cobain holding baby Frances Bean in which he's wearing a T-shirt that reads *Grunge is dead*, a sentiment people later called prophetic. But I guess I was proof that the music didn't die after all.

I hadn't responded to Obe's message. He wasn't one for sentiment or wordiness, but I could not risk telling him anything or I might tell him everything. I needed to find Janey Keogh. I knew, despite my uneven upbringing, that it was rude to show up unannounced on Christmas Day, but I had been waiting a long time.

By the time I made it to North Vancouver, there was a light dusting of snow on the ground, which is uncommon enough to send us West Coasters into a panic. I pulled up to the house in a yellow taxi, because public transit only took me so far. By then, it was four p.m. and already falling dark. The cabdriver, wearing a blue-and-white Canucks scarf, seemed nervous having me in his car. He was visibly relieved when I handed him the cash, a big chunk of the money from Aunt Gillian, and then he sped away.

Janey Keogh lived in a small town house with a wooden porch that slanted like a smirk. There was a single string of white Christmas lights wound around the porch rail, and a stroller by the front door. Lights glowed behind the curtains. For one heartbeat I considered not going in, not disturbing the scene, which seemed as cozy as the inside of a snow globe. Then I leaned on the doorbell as if I were on the stoop bleeding from a gunshot wound.

Through the window, I saw a girl my age dressed entirely in pink, standing on one leg and talking on a cell phone. She glanced at the door, annoyed, and cracked it open. I heard overflow noise from a TV, a *boing-boing* sound like a cartoon, and a child howling.

"I'll call you back in a sec. Someone's here," the girl said into the phone, and then she stared at me.

"Yeah?" she asked, by way of greeting. "Are you collecting for something? I don't have money." I focused on her silver nose ring, even though it wasn't a novelty. Half my school had one. I hadn't pictured this scenario. I had imagined Janey, alone, ready to take all my questions.

"Janey?" My doorbell ringing had been belligerent, but my vocal cords collapsed when I tried to speak. I knew she wasn't Janey, of course. Janey would be entering middle age.

"Um, *no-oh*," the girl said, as if saying *duh*.

"Can I come in?" It was clear this chick was not going

to extend the invitation, even though I was standing in the freezing cold.

"State your business," she quipped, which seemed like something she'd heard in a movie. She ignored the shouts from another room, two kids' voices. She was obviously used to tuning it out.

"I'm Nico. I just came in from Victoria," I said, tugging off my hat. I took a big step into the hall. Wet snow slapped on the floor. "My mom knew your mom."

I felt a wave of dizziness saying "mom" twice in one sentence. It was a word I avoided.

"Angela, but I go by Ange. And she is not my mother. She's my stepmother, and an evil one. She leaves me with the brats all the time."

"You have a sister?" I had so wanted a sister.

"One stepsister, one stepbrother," she said, eyeing her phone. I was not interesting enough to keep her from her conversation. "They're watching *Frosty* or some shit like that."

She put one hand on her hip, which was covered in hot-pink velour. It was likely a knockoff of those super-pricey tracksuits girls had sold kidneys for. Her brown hair was swept back by a headband with silver rhinestones. She wore enormous matching rhinestone-studded hoop earrings, so I knew she'd thought about her ensemble even though she was trying to look as if she hadn't.

"I need to talk to your mother. Will she be home soon?"

"She's not my fucking mother!"

"Okay, Ange, but can you let me wait inside?" I asked,

leaning on her name. "It's taken me hours to get here and I'm fucking freezing." I kicked off my boots, which splattered grimy slush on the tiles. I was staying.

"Fine, whatever you said your name is, come in, but you can't do drugs here."

"What? Are you kidding?" I followed her into the small sitting room at the front of the house. She gripped her phone like a barbell and sat down in a leather recliner without inviting me to sit. Did she think I was a street kid? I felt bad about everything. *I hate myself and I want to die,* I thought, trying it on for size. I'm not even sure the words held any meaning. I wondered if that was how Kurt Cobain felt singing the band's big hits over and over.

The house was small and narrow. A dwarf artificial tree decorated with tinsel sat by the front window. Barbie dresses and Lego pieces were scattered like buckshot all over the carpet, along with tangles of ribbons and tumbleweeds of wrapping paper. There was a square glass coffee table, a sofa covered with a crocheted blanket, and a gray suede armchair. On the table was a plate with cookie crumbs on it and an empty mug. I realized it was the remnants of milk and cookies for Santa, left out the night before. I sat on the sofa, which sighed under my weight. The noise had stopped.

"You want to check on the kids?"

"No. They're fine. You say your mom knows Janey?"

"Knew. My mom's dead."

"Shit, are you talking about Annalee?" She leaned forward, her phone sliding along the pink velour and onto the floor. "Janey told me about her. She named my stepsister, Lila, after her. The middle name, anyway."

I took a deep breath, inhaling a meaty smell from the kitchen. A roast. I decided to let her talk.

"Was she really . . . you know . . ."

"Was she really murdered?" Ange was pissing me off. Even the fact that she called herself Ange was pissing me off. Where was Janey, anyway? It was Christmas, for God's sake. Ange had a gold necklace that spelled out *Angel* in swirly script, and that annoyed me, too. She'd probably shoplifted it. "We don't know. She was never found," I told her.

"So creepy," she pronounced, and gave a shiver, as if she'd tasted something bitter. "Janey said your mom was her best friend. She said she'd find you one day."

One day. I had lived in the same house my whole life.

"Well, I made it easier for her. When's she coming back?"

"Any time now. She's out with my dad getting a scooter for Lila. Jason got one, so Lila needs one, too. Everything has to be fair."

"Yeah."

"Janey was a wild child, or so my dad says. She pretends to be goody-goody now, but for sure she, like, got into the hard stuff when she lived in Puerto Rico." Ange widened her eyes, letting her news sink in.

"Oh yeah? Your dad told you that?" I rubbed at a worn patch on the armrest. I still wore the bandages where I'd hurt my hand on the ferry. They were puckered and curling up at the sides like cooked bacon.

"He hinted. I think it was supposed to be a warning. Hugs-not-drugs deal. He only gets me half time, so he tries to make it count before I go back to my mom."

"Been there," I said, which wasn't true, but I wanted her to keep talking. "What else did she say about my mother?"

"Did you know they went to a Nirvana concert? Janey showed me a photo. Oh God, Kurt Cobain. *Sooo* beautiful."

I tensed, my body going into alert at the mention of Nirvana and Cobain. There was more mewling from the basement, and a call of "Ange! Come quick, the TV is broken."

"They always do this. Try to change the channel on their own. They're going to start fighting in three, two, one . . ." She sighed and got up, her track pants flapping as she went.

Either the smell of the meat cooking made me sick or I didn't like to hear her talk about Cobain, because I felt faint, like I had at the cabin. I stood up and headed to the hall, thinking I'd gulp some air. I walked right into Janey. She wore a cherry-red coat and clutched a massive plastic bag. She absorbed my knit hat, my unwashed blue hair sticking out of it, and my packs on the floor. None of it looked good.

Her light brown hair was pulled away from her face into a messy bun. She peered at me from behind black-rimmed glasses: square frames, hipster style.

"Can I help you?" she asked. "Are you a friend of Angela's?" She scrutinized me, as if judging that to be unlikely.

"Are you Janey Keogh?" I asked, even though I knew she was. I heard feet thumping up stairs.

"I was. Before I was married. And who are you?" The tone was becoming less friendly.

A child started screaming "Mom-*MEE*!"

"I'm Nico—Nicola. Annalee's daughter," I said, my voice trembling on the last word.

"My God," she said. "You've grown up."

I stood in the hall, waiting. A red-haired child, probably three or four, appeared at Janey's side and leaned against her hip, claiming her. The girl had Hello Kitty barrettes fastened by each ear. Tears streaked her face.

Janey whispered to the girl. I heard "basement" and "TV," and whatever she said must have been satisfactory, because the girl trundled off, giving me one last cold glance.

"She can go watch TV with her brother," Janey said, explaining as if I were an inspector from social services. What did I care? Why did mothers with young children always think everyone cared whether they fed their kids organic or what ballet school they chose? I was left alone plenty of times as a little girl, more than I could count. Besides, the kid had already been watching TV, possibly for hours, given that Angela was in charge.

"I guess Angela showed you in," she said, tucking a lock of hair behind her ear. "Let me take off my coat. My husband's just gone to get some whipping cream. He'll be right back."

I was clearly making her nervous. I walked back into the sitting room.

"Have a seat, Nico-*lah*," she said, gesturing to the armchair. "Excuse the mess."

Jesus. She had avoided me for ten years and now she was worried about what I thought of her housekeeping?

"Can you call me Nico?" I asked, my voice hoarse.

"I haven't seen you since you were tiny," Janey said, sitting stiffly in her chair and looking cornered.

"Uh-huh." I kicked a piece of Lego away. I was suddenly not feeling so grown-up. Her whole house smelled like a family: the cookies, the roast, and the powdery plastic smell of new toys.

"I always meant to find you. To talk."

Ange walked in, phone to ear, saw us together, and walked out again, no doubt to eavesdrop.

"I've been in the same place for fifteen years."

"I'm not sure now is the time for this talk," she said stiffly. "It's Christmas."

Right. I had failed to notice.

"What I mean is, we've got guests coming. They don't know about my past."

"I won't stay long." I waited. I forced myself to look her in the eye.

"It was a bit . . . complicated. Your father didn't like me. He thought I was a bad influence. I did drugs," she said, whispering the last part. "I don't want Angela to know."

Of course, Angela already knew. Parents could be so clueless. I felt as if we were in an elevator together and she was going to exit at a different floor. I had to sprint to the important questions.

"What was my mother like?"

She thought for a moment, gazing up at the white stucco on the ceiling as if the words hung there.

"She was like my sister. What can I say? She was beautiful, but you know that. She was gentle to others but tough on herself. You know her own parents died young. What else . . ." Janey removed her glasses and wiped the corner of her eye.

"Music. She loved music. Annalee looked sweet, those brown eyes, but she liked loud, badass music and she hated unfairness. She loved mountains, and we joked about being ski bums together in Whistler even though she didn't ski. She never drove, either, but she loved riding her bike."

I wondered if Janey had rehearsed this over the years. What she would say to me.

"We still have her bike," I interjected flatly. "It's somewhere in our shed." It was a touring bike with only three gears, and it needed a tune-up. The suspension was off. Still, I should have had it fixed and ridden it. Her wicker basket decorated with plastic flowers was still attached to the front.

"And you. Nico, she loved you. She was scared to become a mom, but you should have seen her just after you were born. She couldn't stop smiling."

There was a bump downstairs from Janey's basement. A kid screeched. Time was running out. Janey sighed, a tear spilling down her cheek.

"She was young, Nico. She had no parents to help her, and Verne was working all the time. She became . . .

confused. I was out of town when you were little, and I couldn't visit much. Besides, Verne didn't like me staying too long."

"Why?"

"Well, I did the things that young people do, for one. I think that's something you should ask your dad. But, Nico . . ."

"Yeah?"

"If Annalee said she was coming back for you, she was. I have never met anyone more determined. She never had much money, and she had to fight to get her parents cared for when they got sick, first her mother, then her father. She had some rough breaks."

"And then she got stuck with me. You don't need to tell me, Janey. I know I was an accident. That's been clear all my life."

"You were a happy accident, Nico. But your parents had problems. You really need to talk to your dad."

An oven timer went off in the kitchen. Janey let it ding. I had so many more questions. I wanted to know how my mother did her hair, if she liked art.

"Do you have any idea where she might have been going? She said she would be back."

"You know the police asked me all that. And Verne did, too. I doubt she'd have traveled that far. I couldn't think of anywhere she would have gone, not for long. Not without you."

"But you could imagine her going without Verne?"

"I'm biased about Verne. After Annalee disappeared, he

asked me not to speak to you. He made me promise. Nico, I'm so sorry. I've thought about you all the time. And I think of Annalee, of course. I still miss her. She had this jingly laugh."

I looked at Janey and I believed her, sort of, but she clearly had a job and kids and a husband and roasts to check and new friends she met at yoga and all kinds of busy, busy to fill in the cracks, the questions, and the fears about Annalee. I just had cracks.

"There's never been—" she started.

"No, no body. No suspects. No nothing."

"Nico, I haven't offered you anything. Are you hungry? Verne does know you're here, right?" Her black-framed glasses sat slightly off-kilter.

"Yes. . . . We're staying at a hotel downtown. Little Christmas holiday from Victoria."

"I have to admit, Nico. I still can't make sense of it, even after all these years. She was so *good*. I mean she sometimes had a temper, but that's because she cared about things."

"Did she love Kurt Cobain?"

"Who didn't?" said Janey, giving a hoarse laugh. Then she talked about how my mother liked vintage things and was pretty hopeless with technology, like burning CDs. "If it had been up to her, we'd all still be listening to vinyl," she said with a sad smile.

I heard the front door open, boots stamping, a closet opening, and then Janey's husband appeared wearing a cable-knit sweater that looked fresh from the department store. He held a plastic grocery bag.

"I got the last whipping cream in the Lower Mainland," he said, and then noticed me. Janey introduced us, but he still looked confused, as if the seams of Christmas were being pulled out right before his eyes. Then the two kids ran after him, the red-haired girl and an older boy, who eyed me suspiciously. I was outnumbered.

The doorbell rang, and the husband, Robert or Roger, opened the door to two silver-haired grandparents carrying bags of more presents. A breeze of sweet floral perfume surfed in on the cold air. There was Roger (or Robert) and Margaret and Kent and I couldn't keep track of everyone. They were all watching, waiting for me to explain myself and to leave, or preferably just leave.

"This is Nicola," Janey told everyone. "She's Annalee's daughter."

The children blinked at me. The grandparents were confused and then concerned, perhaps at my tangled blue hair. Roger/Robert frowned, no doubt wondering if there would be enough places at the dinner table.

"I can't stay," I shouted above the din, making my way to the door. "I have somewhere to be."

I struggled into my boots. Janey held up my jacket. There was a small tear on the elbow that I needed to have patched. I was wearing the vintage floral-print dress again, but it was wrinkled and seemed faded and cheap. The drab clothes of a poor person, not someone with a keen eye for something vintage made with care. Ange joined the crowd, as if on cue, probably wanting to see how the evening was going to play out. Her grandmother grabbed her and drew her into a tight embrace, setting off another wave of perfume.

"We're going to a nice restaurant," I said loudly. No one asked which one; possibly because nobody believed me. The others retreated to the living room. Janey waited. I had one more question. "What was her favorite Nirvana song?"

"All of them," Janey said. "Did you know she once had blue hair, too? Streaks, just for a few days."

"Yeah?" I zipped my jacket. Tugged my cap back on. One of the children was screaming again, some dispute over the new gifts.

I shouldered my packs and turned to the door.

"Nico? I'll say this. Early days? 'Sliver.' Later, it was 'All Apologies,' the melody. She actually used to sing it to you."

"Thanks, Janey." I was grateful that she didn't wish me a Merry Christmas. "Sliver," of course, is one of the songs where Cobain shows he knows how much a kid can hurt. The boy desperately wants to go home and says he wants to be alone, but I think really he wanted his mother. At the end of the song, the boy wakes up in his mother's arms.

CHAPTER 13

"TERRITORIAL PISSINGS"

If there were a pie chart showing survey results to the question "What is your favorite Nirvana song?" you'd find a big slice devoted to "Lithium." There's something about it. The song begins with Kurt saying he's so happy. The bass makes you think of someone sneaking around, tiptoe-ing. By the time it gets to the serrated-edge "yeahs," you can't help but toss your head back and forth. I was thinking about "Lithium" while I sat on a Vancouver bus, listening to my CD player.

The holiday schedule made it an agonizing trip from North Vancouver to Delta and the ferry terminal. The final push took us past shadowy farmers' fields that in the summer would produce blueberries but in winter looked stark and foreboding. I exhaled when we hit the causeway, the ocean unfurling on either side. The manmade causeway punched into the ocean like an outstretched arm making a fist. We were almost there.

I stepped off the city bus and faced the slap of freezing air, feeling relief and even a pinch of pride. I had made it that far. I would be early for the 10:45 p.m. sailing for Duke Point. Then I'd find my way back to Cobain's cabin, somehow.

I approached the ticket counter, putting on my friendly face, or giving it a try. I had my hair tucked under my hat again. Then the mannish woman at the ticket booth kindly told me that there were no more ferries that night to Duke Point. That 10:45 ferry I was counting on ran almost every night except Christmas. And I'd missed the nine p.m. sailing from Vancouver to Victoria by just two minutes.

"Next sailing to Duke Point is at five-fifteen a.m. tomorrow. You have someone to pick you up, honey?" the woman asked, flashing me a stiff smile. I often feared people in uniform, even a BC Ferries worker. It was irrational. Verne wore a uniform, after all.

"Yes," I said, and turned away. "They're in the parking lot, waiting to make sure I get on." I was getting good at lying. That was the kind of thing relatives did, right? Saw you safely on board? Change of plans; I guess I'll have to sleep on the spare bed after all.

"Merry Christmas," I remembered to say to the woman, still playing my part.

"And you, too, dear." She slid the window shut.

I could feel the tears coming, so I whacked myself on the cheek. What would the young Cobain have done? He'd play his guitar until security came and told him to stop. Then he'd play some more. The terminal's main commercial building, the Tsawwassen Quay Market, was like a well-lit airplane hangar, with shops selling pricey organic coffee, gelato, and fudges. It was closed for the night. I was alone and freezing at the end of a three-kilometer manmade causeway, surrounded by water. It would be the perfect night to jump to escape. I could just slip into the ocean as if it were layers of cold black silk.

My other option was finding a place to hunker down for the night. There was the long stretch of beach on the causeway, but it was exposed and the winds were high, the temperature frigid. No tent and no sleeping bag, and my toes were already numb in my boots. I knew one thing for sure: I had to keep moving or security would be after me.

I walked toward the parking lot, the muscles between my shoulders already throbbing. I marched for about fifteen minutes, trying to look as if I had somewhere to go. I stopped, unzipped my backpack, and took out a men's wool sweater (thrift-store special) and a pair of wool skate socks. I yanked these on quickly, trying to avoid the car headlights flashing past. *Don't cry.* I tried to think of a song to calm my nerves, landed on John Denver, "Rocky Mountain High."

I had to stay hidden from cops looking for a missing girl. The beaches were dark and shadowy. The rocks and driftwood resembled something on an X-ray, and I could hear the waves punching the shore. Putting my boots back on, I saw two figures huddled on the beach around a small fire of driftwood. One of them was shouting, as if trying to be heard over the roar of his drunkenness. I zipped my jacket up. I had packed for a city jaunt staying at a Seattle condo, not sleeping rough outdoors.

One night. I could survive one night. Had my mother done this? Slept alone, swallowed by the cold? *No, don't think about that. Keep walking.* Something whipped against my leg, and I nearly cried out. It was a black garbage bag, which I kept, tucking it under my chest straps. I wore my knapsack in front, which made me wobbly.

My eyes watered. The wind scraped over the sand, making a high-pitched wail. I could see shapes bobbing on the water, likely buoys or deadheads, but I thought of bloated bodies.

I hate myself and I want to die.

Kurt Cobain was always threatening to use that line as an album title. I wondered where he was, if he was waiting for me. Perhaps he had even figured out who I was. I had almost thought of him as "my Cobain" but caught myself.

I could see by a streetlight that there was some kind of structure at the edge of the beach, near the parking lot. Someone had made a lean-to out of driftwood, a rough A-frame. It was far back enough from the water to offer wind protection.

There was no one in sight. The wind nearly snatched my hat, so I knelt down, and spread out the garbage bag in the lean-to. It was dry and didn't smell, which was a good sign. After climbing out, I felt the first drops of cold rain hit my shoulder. My backpack wasn't going to fit, so I set it next to the lean-to. If I got wet, I'd freeze to death. I knew that much. I tossed my knapsack down in the lean-to to use as a pillow and crawled in.

The wind whipped through the gaps in the wood. It was like lying in a rib cage. Cars and trucks still passed now and then. At least I was hidden from the road. If I was caught, I wouldn't get to see Cobain again. I couldn't risk that. I tried closing my eyes. The wind sounded like a feral dog howling. Something thwacked against the shelter, maybe a beer can. I pressed the light on my watch: It was only ten-thirty. Still Christmas. *Zut alors*, I thought, which made me smile, thinking of Cobain and his strange ways.

10:33 p.m. I was freezing. I thought maybe I should just keep moving, keep walking, but the rain was heavy. I needed someone to tell me what to do. I closed my eyes again, hugging myself.

A couple more cars passed. Then there was just the sound of the wind meeting the ocean, like a knife being sharpened. The ocean is not peaceful. It tosses and wails. I didn't hear the footsteps. I heard the shouting. A figure crawling into the lean-to, two hands pressing against my shoulders, pinning me to the ground.

"This is my fuckin' house. My fuckin' house." His face was over mine. A whiff of the dirty ochre smell of old nicotine. I could see only by the cracks of white from the streetlight shining through the wood. His nose appeared lumpy, as if fashioned from clay. He pressed harder on my shoulders. Thumped me once against the sand. My head bounced. I heard ringing in my ears, and I realized: I was already in a coffin. I tried to push him off, but it was as if a Dumpster had overturned on me.

His knees were on either side of me, and he leaned forward, wringing the air from my rib cage. *I will die on the beach*, I thought. *Here, on Christmas Day*. The life was being squeezed from me. It was not how I had pictured dying.

I pounded my hands together to make one fist, like in volleyball. I thrust my hands up, one sharp movement, as if swinging an axe. My fist hit his nose.

"Whore!" he yelled, grabbing at his face. I raised my knee to his stomach and he was off me. I stomped and flailed my way out of the lean-to, as if doing a furious backstroke in the sand.

The man crawled out and snatched at me as I grabbed my knapsack, his lank brown hair whipping in the wind. I raced up to the sidewalk, swinging my bag on my back. Sprinting down the highway, I heard him shouting, and I heard the wind and the buzz of my own blood rushing.

Snowdrops are kind of a sad flower, because sometimes, like the robins, they come back too soon. They think it's spring, so they nudge out, only to be smacked down by another frost.

After Kurt Cobain died, Krist Novoselic and Dave Grohl eventually had to go on with their lives. Novoselic played bass in other bands, became active in politics, and married his second wife, an artist. Grohl founded the band the Foo Fighters, and people asked, "Who knew?" because Grohl sang and wrote songs and played guitar as well as drums. He did it all well.

A crater opened up when Cobain supposedly shot himself. People tried to fill it in with vigils, and merchandise, and tribute songs, and there were bad, tasteless jokes, because nobody knows how to behave in the face of tragedy. People standing inside a crater, like me after my mother disappeared, have to act like they're okay so everything else can carry on. I did; otherwise, who could stand to look at me? Me, the girl with the mother who might have been a druggie, or murdered, or God knows what. Me, the girl whose dad trimmed her bangs too short and made crooked braids. That girl.

I ran down Highway 17, and if the few passing motorists noticed me, they didn't slow, even for a girl on the road alone at eleven p.m. on Christmas. After a few minutes I was out of breath and realized that no one was going to stop me. I remembered then about the headlamp Verne had given me, dug it out of my knapsack, and pulled it over my head. It was tight around my forehead. Was that what the beginning of a migraine felt like? The causeway stretched behind me like an exposed spine. No one was following. I came to a turnoff for Tsawwassen Drive North and kept jogging, my feet still moving, my blood still pumping, the headlamp casting its beam along the rural road. I wondered if I was on the reserve yet, the Tsawwassen First Nation land. I heard a rustle in the bushes and scanned around with the headlamp. Cougars attack from behind, I had read. They were elite predators. I slowed to a walk, gasping. Running makes you look like prey.

The fear seemed to reconnect the dial-up to my brain, and I remembered: my big backpack was sitting against the lean-to. Its contents would no doubt be gone. My clothes were gone, a gift I'd bought for Verne, and . . . the CDs. My mother's CDs. Carefully surrounded by my socks and underwear to make sure they weren't damaged. Stupid. Stupid. Stupid. I thought about going back for them.

But I was not that brave, or crazy. Instead I cried, and tears ran down my jacket as I walked along the shoulder past rancher homes that had seen better days. After what seemed like hours, I came to a narrow white church with a white cross at the top of the steeple. My whole body shook with cold as I went around to the front doors, brown, with two white crosses. I considered sleeping under the steps but settled into a rusted old boat sitting next to the church. The boat was beached, probably forever, and left to decay. At some point I stopped crying. I shivered the whole night through.

Lying in the starless black, I inhaled the smell of salt and wet rust and tried to summon a memory of my mother, but the one I pulled out was hazy. I could picture myself sitting in a yellow swing, and Verne giving me a push while Annalee held a camera and waved. No, that wasn't it. There was a photo of us by the yellow swing. I couldn't invent the memories. They had to be real. All I wanted was to sleep and not think, ever again, but my body was too cold to succumb.

At four a.m., I strapped the headlamp back on to walk, stiff-legged, to the highway. I saw tall, shadowy figures standing by the church. Totem poles. I shined the headlamp on a stone plaque in the earth marking the Tsawwassen Indian reserve, circa 1879, and the Church of the Holy Ghost, built in 1904.

I dreamed of hot coffee as I trudged. My nail beds had turned opal blue, and my legs throbbed with fatigue. I couldn't believe I had walked so far in the dark, all on a tidal wave of fear and adrenaline. When I reached the lean-to it was empty, but there were prints all around from my boots and his. I shined the headlamp on the sand next to the lean-to. There was a depression, as if an animal had nestled there. My backpack and all its contents were gone. He had taken it as compensation for my time in his "house." And I could never report it.

I staggered onto the ferry, almost too burned out to care if I was identified. Perhaps the 5:15 a.m. to Nanaimo was not on the radar. I just wanted to get back to Cobain. I wanted his help. I *needed* his help. Verne would say no, but Cobain was crazy enough to agree. The coffee from the ferry vending machines tasted as if it were made from pennies and hot water. I tried to pry my mind away from those missing CDs. My fists kept clenching.

Would Sean still like me if he saw me like this? Did he really like me at all? He wasn't muscle-bound, but he looked fit and strong. He probably could have dealt with the guy on the beach and gotten my pack back. On the other hand, he might have already forgotten about me.

Or had a girlfriend he didn't mention. He didn't seem like someone with a girlfriend, but that was what some dudes did, right?

I bought a packaged cookie the size of a Frisbee from the vending machine, and the sugar hurtled into my bloodstream. I could feel my body rumbling back to life. I tried to think about Sean—that was what girls did, right? But I kept wondering about Obe. I fished out my cell phone and started dialing his number, an action as familiar as brushing my teeth. It rang and rang, the curling sound penetrating my eardrums. Where was he? Did he not know I needed to hear his voice?

Of course Obe wasn't there. He was in Winnipeg with his family, hopefully not waiting for his dad to call. Sometimes his dad tried to get in touch around the holidays, and it didn't always go well. It was worse when his dad forgot, though. And worse yet when Obe's dad talked to Nadia. Obe's mother was all butterscotch and sunshine to everyone except Obe's father, and with good reason.

Not being able to talk to Obe made me lonelier. When we docked, I stood near a family of six and tried to appear as if I were with them and all their bumping tote bags and hand-holding and fussing kids. At least I was less conspicuous without my big backpack.

I had become the textbook teenage runaway, standing at the ice-cobbled roadside with my dirty hair and my outstretched thumb. It took about an hour, but a station wagon that resembled a brown bread box on wheels slowed and stopped. The man and the woman were on their way from Courtenay, up Island, to visit their daughter in Victoria. They were settled into that midpoint of life when people get rounded and soft, before their edges sharpen and they become brittle with age. The couple was listening to a Top 40 radio station broadcasting some kind of best-of-the-ages countdown. The man tapped his hand on the steering wheel as he drove.

"You really shouldn't hitchhike, dear. Not everyone is friendly folk like us."

I murmured my agreement. "I didn't want my grandma behind the wheel today, what with the ice," I said. "You can drop me off up ahead. Her drive is pretty rough, and I don't want y'all getting stuck."

Y'all? I said "y'all" now?

"We don't want to leave you by the roadside," said the man, Dave or something. I had forgotten.

"No, no, it's fine. Look, the sun is even kind of shining." Light was struggling to push through the steel-wool clouds. It was still cold, but the wind had died down. Just then, the radio played "Smells Like Teen Spirit," and I expected Mr. Dave to turn it off, but he just kept tapping his hand on the wheel. He'd no doubt heard it hundreds of times in grocery stores and shopping malls. The backseat was crammed with presents in festive gift bags with buttons and ribbons. There was an oblong baking pan covered in foil, then wrapped again in several layers of plastic. Clearly, these people had not gotten the memo from the environment.

The woman had a paperback splayed open on her lap,

the same silver-and-blue one everyone had been reading on the ferry: *A Time to Cry*. It was hard not to shake my head to "Smells Like Teen Spirit." Sure, it was a megahit. I still liked it. Kurt Cobain had no idea that Teen Spirit was the name of a girl's deodorant when he wrote that song. Kathleen Hanna, lead singer for the band Bikini Kill, had sprayed *Kurt Smells Like Teen Spirit* on the wall of his apartment. Cobain was dating Bikini Kill's drummer, Tobi Vail, at the time and was quite smitten. In fact, his love even made him sick, or so he wrote in "Aneurysm."

I jumped out of the car and waved, just as "Teen Spirit" was ending. I continued to wave, keen as a cheerleader, as they pulled away. They had called me dear. I was already planning to tell Cobain about them and the man on the beach. Cobain would say he'd warned me about that kind of thing, which was true, but how was I to know that the ferry wasn't running? I walked down the country road, trying to figure out my way back to the cabin. The trip to Vancouver had been a nightmare, all in all, but it was done. I was ready to confront Cobain and use whatever emotional blackmail I could to secure his help.

My boots crunched on the ice patches that had formed over the mud. The storm on the mainland the night before had obviously hit Vancouver Island as well. Big branches swept over the road like green shawls. If the road had a sign somewhere, I couldn't see it. Cobain had called it simply Nameless Road. There were tire tracks in the thin dusting of snow. Someone had come or gone. I wondered if Cobain had company.

The cabin seemed sturdier from the outside, hewn together with thick, smooth logs. The gravel drive ended at
the cabin, and there were no neighbors in sight, nothing
but trees. The birds peeped, flitting cautiously about the
way they do the morning after a storm.

I rapped on the door, hard, thinking that Cobain could
still be asleep. He was known to be lazy in matters pertain-
ing to anything but music. I pounded again, growing impatient. After all I'd been through, he could at least open
the door.

"Come on, Cobain. Wake up."

Shit, I had said it. Cobain. There was silence except for
snow melting off the trees and onto the ground, a slow,
soft sound like a hand being patted. I went around to the
side of the cabin and noticed an empty wooden crate by
the woodshed. I positioned it under the bathroom window, which was high above the toilet. The window slid
open with three or four hard blows with the side of my
bandaged hand. Caulking and other pieces of debris rained
down. I lowered myself backward and managed to get both
boots on either side of the toilet lid.

I could see right away that Cobain had left his turtles
behind, which meant he was coming back. He did love the
turtles. I wondered what they ate and if I could feed them.
I opened the medicine cabinet, but all I found were pills,
and lots of them: orange ones, blue ones, and white ones,
all in prescription bottles. All them were prescribed to different people, including a couple made out to John Simon
Ritchie. None of them were made out to a Daniel. I wasn't

educated enough about pills to know what the medicines treated or what they did to you. I could see no methadone. You usually had to go to a clinic every day for that. I'd learned that much living in my neighborhood.

When I went into the main part of the cabin, things didn't look right. Cobain's laptop sat on the table with the lid pulled down but not shut. It glowed and ebbed slightly, as if it were sentient but dozing. A brown paper cup of shitty convenience-store coffee sat next to it. Couldn't Cobain even make his own coffee? I touched the cup. It was full but cold. Cobain had left in a hurry. I placed my hands on the silver top of his computer and lifted the case, slowly, as if checking under a manhole. He'd been in the middle of writing something.

He realized then that he was going to have to kill her. The days had grown long and bloated, and he had put off the task long enough. He paused for a second and wound up his toy monkey, which always helped him think. How to do it was the question. His bag of tricks was nearly empty.

I heard the door latch rattle and slammed the computer closed, jumping up.

"Nico, what the fuck?" said Cobain. He was wearing the hunting cap again. He had also broken out long johns and boarder shorts, an outfit that suggested he had taken some of the pills in the cabinet. "What the fuck?" seemed to be Cobain's version of *"Que pasa?"* so I answered accordingly.

175

"I just got back from Vancouver now. I had to stay overnight, missed the last ferry." I backed away from the computer toward the kitchen knives. Cobain had always written disturbing things in his diaries, I knew; I had read *about* them, if not the actual journals. These days, he was using a laptop instead of a Mead notebook. I knew he couldn't have been writing about me. They were just words, a dark story, like the song "Polly," about a woman who is abducted and tortured, although that was inspired by a real case Cobain heard about in the news.

"You stayed with that Janey friend in North Van? Did she have any answers?"

He swung his right arm around and produced a carton of plain doughnut holes, the kind that look like golden golf balls.

"No, not really. I thought you had gone." I was still shaken. He might have left for good. Then how would I find him?

"I thought *you* had disappeared. You said you'd be back, so I was worried. But I did buy you a coffee. Hmm, I left it in the car."

Cobain disappeared out the door. I flipped the laptop up.

Today was the day, he thought, feeling neither melancholic nor euphoric. It simply was. The time had come.

I closed it again. I must have looked guilty.

"Shit, I left that on. I had to go make a phone call. I wasn't getting cell reception again. It comes and goes."

"Who were you calling?"

"Someone I know."

"Figured that."

"Did the trip help?"

"Not really. Sort of."

"So now what?"

"I need you to help me find my mother."

"What? I can't keep doing this Nancy Drew stuff. I have deadlines. And I'm not a very nice man."

"You don't have to be nice. Please. No one's really helped me before. They've just told me lies. I feel like I could . . . find her."

"We need to call the police," he declared, enunciating as if he were auditioning for a play.

"Okay, how do you think that will go for us?"

"Nico, I could go to prison as a child abductor."

"Please help me. You're smarter than the cops. We'll be careful," I said, trying to appeal to his vanity and his dislike of cops.

He considered, rubbing the stubble on his chin. Tears tugged at my eyes, which were the same color blue as his, but not lit from behind like his.

"Then, after, I'll go. I won't bother you anymore." I was counting on Cobain having one of his mood swings.

"That will be it?"

"Yes. That will be the end."

"Okay, *andiamo*," he said. "Right after we feed the turtles."

CHAPTER 14

"ANEURYSM"

When everyone was writing off Kurt Cobain as a junkie and pretty much sticking a fork in Nirvana, Cobain fired back at his critics by kicking off their set at the Reading Festival in a wheelchair, wearing a fright wig and a hospital gown. Some critics had predicted he wouldn't even show up. By all accounts, the show was electrifying. Cobain had come back swinging, and so would I. The bad news was that he and I would have to catch a ferry, which would be risky.

"I don't know if you've noticed, Nico, but I'm not a burly man. I would not do well in prison." Cobain twitched a bit as he drove. I wondered if he had an actual driver's license. He wore big white-framed sunglasses, as if that were a real disguise.

He flipped on the radio to the news channel. Manic ads

for Boxing Day sales. Power outages due to the storm, and a public appeal for information on one Nicola Cavan, age fifteen, missing since Christmas Eve. I was officially gone, but it was unclear whether I'd fled or been taken.

"Oh, *scheisse!*" said Cobain. "We've got to go back. This is serious." He said that, yet kept driving to the ferry terminal.

"I'll hide in the trunk. No one will see me. I'll stay in the car the whole ferry ride if I have to. I will. I'll stay in the fucking trunk."

"Nico, I am making a mistake here. And I'm doing this for one reason only: I don't want you to go alone, and I know you will." He thought for a second. "The other reason is because I have a daughter about your age."

I knew better than to point out that he'd given two reasons, or maybe to him they were really the same. He stared at me hard and then cranked up the Pixies. Here comes your man.

He demanded that I stay in the trunk until we arrived in Vancouver. Maybe he thought the cops wouldn't believe that I'd gone with him of my own free will, and that they would think I had *schadenfreude* or Stockholm syndrome or whatever it was called. I had wanted to get out and email Obe and Sean using the Internet on the ferry, but Cobain forbade it. If we got caught, our mission was aborted. (Actually, he said it would be "fuckered.") The trunk was freezing and dark and smelled like winter boots, moldy rugs, and wet dog. Maybe he'd had the turtles in there. After the first fifteen minutes, I got freaked out, so I hummed softly to myself like some of the homeless people do.

Cobain had gone into the passenger lounge and the warm cafeteria. "If you get a Nanaimo bar, you'd better get me one," I told him. I was really in no position to make demands, though.

Once we'd rolled off the ferry and cleared the terminal, Cobain let me out of the trunk and into the backseat, where I was to lie down. We listened to the news as he negotiated his way through the downtown core. He seemed a nervous driver. Of course, I was used to being in a car with Verne, who was cautious but confident. Cobain drove too slowly, which I knew was also a hazard. Cars honked. Vancouver had a high ranking for bad traffic, and I wished Cobain would step on the gas. We couldn't afford to attract attention. While he fiddled with the radio, I wondered if I should tell him about the older man in the station wagon who gave me the ride, and how he kept time to "Smells Like Teen Spirit." No, he wouldn't think it was funny. Plus, Cobain was getting old. Older. I wondered if he had a hang-up about turning forty, which would be soon—in February. I wondered if he secretly saw his daughter. I mean, his other daughter.

Maybe there was some way he could reclaim his fortune. His fingerprints and dental records would be on file, and the authorities could test, what, his DNA? Many fans, some of Cobain's circle of friends, Cobain's grandfather, and even a determined private investigator believed that his death was murder, questioning how someone could ingest as much heroin as he did and still pull the trigger of a shotgun. And why were there no fingerprints on it? It might not be that hard for Cobain to convince the authorities that he was alive. It would get the conspiracy theorists to back off Courtney Love, at least. Most of the stories made her seem pretty *coco loco*, but if she'd made Cobain happy, who was to judge? As long as she didn't try to stop me from seeing him, I had no problem with her. And Frances. She was beautiful. I wanted to meet her so badly, in Seattle or Los Angeles, wherever she was. Then she would have a sister and I would have a sister. We would have each other. How had Cobain kept this all secret? Anything was possible, right? Anything was possible if you had heaps of money.

I could only dream about what it would be like to have the kind of money Cobain had, or once had. "We do fine," Verne would say, except he didn't have to eat the toast and runny peanut butter at the school breakfast club, or wear secondhand boots with another kid's name on the heels in marker. Or wonder how you could ever hope to go to art school when there were no savings. How you could even ever *hope*. Funny, there's a place in British Columbia called Hope. It had a big-time natural disaster, a landslide, in the 1960s. People died. Then, years later, the first of the Rambo action movies was filmed there, and that became the other thing that brought the town fame.

"Nico, listen!" Cobain had finally settled on a radio

station. I hadn't seen him wash, brush, or otherwise groom his sandy hair (except raking it with fingers), yet somehow it still looked good.

"No, stay down," he yelled, when I sat up to hear the newscast.

"Nicola Cavan, fifteen, has been missing since Christmas Eve, when she disappeared sometime after leaving the Clipper ferry terminal in downtown Victoria. In the third day of her disappearance, her father, Verne Cavan, is appealing for the public to help find his daughter. 'Please, if you know where she is, pick up the phone. Keep your eyes and ears open. Any information is good information. We want her home. And, Nico: I don't know what you had to do, but just come home. Come home now.'"

Then the female broadcaster talked about my mother, how she went missing at age twenty-eight, leaving me behind. They called my mother a cold case.

"Detective Sergeant Del Stanton, of the Victoria Police, said he has never stopped thinking about the disappearance of Annalee Lester," the reporter said, voice earnest yet smooth, the same neutral tone used to give updates on the stock market.

Then a recording of the officer, Stanton: "She was young and beautiful, and she had a lot of reasons to live, including her little girl, who, on a personal note, is now the same age as my own daughter. We always held hope that new information would bring the pieces together."

The officer sounded as if he was getting choked up at the memory. Why had I never heard of this guy? Then they gave a description of me, complete with the blue hair. Gillian might have emailed some recent photos, too. She had taken a few snapshots in Seattle.

"Nico," said Cobain. "People are really worried. I think it's time you went home."

"No. You promised you'd help me look. It's not too late to tell everyone you kidnapped me. Who would they believe? A helpless girl or a guy with a cabin packed with pills?"

The news report had shaken me. I was talking tough, but my voice quavered. Why hadn't I ever heard about that police detective, Stanton? It was strange that he'd used my mother's maiden name, Lester.

"Those are all prescription meds, Nico. Perfectly legal."

"Yeah, but they're not prescribed for *you*."

"I think I need a hamburger."

We had made it over the Lions Gate Bridge and were heading into West Vancouver. I sighed. I wished he would give up meat once and for all. I desperately had to pee. I'd heard there was construction under way on the Sea-to-Sky Highway to make it safer for the tourists coming to the 2010 Winter Olympics in Whistler. *Please, let the construction be on a Christmas hiatus*, I thought. I was scraping the rind of my patience.

"I'm going to stop in Horseshoe Bay," he said. "There's a stand."

If I asked Cobain how he knew the Vancouver area so well, he'd just lie, so I didn't.

"Stay here," he said.

I waited until he'd parked the Phoenix, crookedly, and left in pursuit of his burger, then bolted from the car, looking for a washroom. I spotted one by the children's playground. There was snow on the ground, a few inches, which I somehow hadn't expected so soon. We were heading up Highway 99, the Sea-to-Sky, en route to Whistler. There would have to be snow at a world-famous ski resort in December.

I lingered at the taps to splash my face and my armpits with water, which only ran icy cold. I badly needed a hot shower and fresh clothes. I was still wearing the floral dress with the men's sweater and black leggings, now torn at the knee.

I'd told Cobain I forgot my backpack on the ferry after seeing Janey, which he'd believed. I was running out of everything. Time. Money. Lies. It was Boxing Day, and pretty soon my regular life would rumble back into action. But I had a feeling my mother had come out this way, and I had to see the area. I'd never traveled down Highway 99, also called the Killer Highway because of all the rockslides and fatal accidents it had witnessed. On one side: rock face; on the other: Howe Sound. Under the bald white light in the women's bathroom I could see my skin was blotchy and greasy. The Kool-Aid dye was fading, leaving strange mottled patches. My eyes were so red that I looked like a speed freak. I dawdled too long, and Cobain beat me back to the Phoenix.

"Nico, get in," he hissed. "What if someone sees you?"

"I'm sorry," I said, getting in the backseat and crouching down. Cars dotted the parking lot, but the cold had driven most travelers inside. There were a few visitors roaming the snowy grounds and snapping photos of the ferries coming in, or of the big brass anchor, which had a plaque to explain some kind of historical significance. "It's probably better not to make a scene, don't you think?"

"Here," he said. "I got you a veggie burger." He passed me a round disk wrapped in foil.

"Thanks. Um, was it cooked right next to your meat burger? Did you see?"

"Shut it," he said, backing up the car in a herky-jerky way. "I said I would take you to Whistler, but we're not staying. Or I'm not. I'll get you there, and then you're on your own."

He cranked up the car radio, which happened to be playing Boston's "More Than a Feeling." The song, the burger with pickles, and being safe in the backseat made me feel happy. There was no one I would rather have been with, except my mother, than crazy Cobain. I think he liked having me there, too.

"Can I move up front now that we've left Vancouver?"

"No," he said, chewing and nodding along to the song. "Too dangerous."

"I need to see the area," I said, in something close to a whine. "That's how I'll know."

Somewhere past Lions Bay (I'd been studying the map during the ferry ride), Cobain stopped the car and let me out.

"You can sit in front," he said. "But wear these." He held out his hunting cap and his big sunglasses. That made me laugh, which annoyed him. While we drove, I thought of myself, of my mother, wondering if she had seen everything I was seeing. A small, less selfish part of me was aware that Cobain was taking a big risk for me.

"So why don't you want to go back? Is your high school that bad?" He turned to me. A scrap of sun shone over Howe Sound, making the highlights in his hair glint and his eyes pop like two topaz marbles.

"You know how bad high school is," I said. "People are simpletons. I once got a detention from a librarian who actually believed my name was Anhedonia. That's a medical term for . . ."

"I know what it means," he mused, shaking his head. He seemed pleased by this story, and smiled. His slender fingers were wrapped loosely around the steering wheel. I wondered if I should remind him that Highway 99 had a rap sheet for being deadly. Cobain was always hunched over, his comma posture even more tragic than my own.

"No, seriously. I told her it was Greek," I said, milking it. The librarian had worn tight burgundy leather pants. She hated kids and had enjoyed using what power she had to hand out detentions. She really should have known the medical term for loss of pleasure in life.

All around us, there were jeeps and vans with chipper bumper stickers, skis strapped to the roof racks, families heading to Whistler for a ski weekend. I knew the Sea-to-Sky Highway was always crawling with people taking off to bike or ski or hike, but not usually with runaway girls trying to find a psychic connection to their missing mothers.

"You're smart, Nico. And you're a pretty good artist. High school's not forever."

"You never told me your real name," I said.

"Huh?"

"Your real name?"

"Daniel Orion." Traffic was growing heavier. People were driving too fast and passing too close. Cobain became agitated, shifting around in his red leather seat. The car smelled of hamburger: pickles, onions, ketchup. He'd thrown his wrapper on the floor.

"Orion, as in the constellation, the hunter?" I thought of the Ouija board's prediction and held my breath.

"No, O'Ryan, as in my ancestors were Irish. You know, drinking and river dancing? Shit. I'm seeing a lot of cop cars around, Nico."

"Let's play a game called Truth," I suggested. "It just involves telling the truth."

"Aren't you supposed to dare as well?"

"I think we're already doing the dare. I'll go first: what do you really do?"

The radio played "My Humps," a massive, ridiculous hit. Cobain scowled, turned it off.

"I don't like to tell people the truth about that."

"Yeah, you some secret agent or something?"

"I write crime novels and people buy them, lots of them. I often base the books on real crimes, so I'm pretty much a literary parasite."

"I've never heard of Daniel O'Ryan," I said.

"If you must know, it's my real name. I write the books under Jasper Jameson. I can't write around other people, or phones, or beeping things, so I hide out; sometimes here, sometimes there."

I remembered all those people on the Clipper ferry reading Jasper Jameson's latest paperback. The guy had an army of followers. Another book was being turned into a movie, I'd heard. The title was something about the dawn.

"You're rich," I said. An accusation. These developments were confusing. The scenery outside the grimy car window appeared phony and sculpted, with the mountains and the ocean seeming to rise before my eyes. It all looked like something from a Greek myth.

"Kind of. Most of it goes to my ex-wife and my daughter. My daughter lives near Seattle. I see her there when my ex-wife lets me. We did not part on good terms, let's say."

I tried to absorb everything he was saying, but my brain was just running white noise. I tried to memorize the cliffs, the islands, and the beaches. Had she been down this highway?

"Now you answer one for me: what are we doing here?"

"I think my mother traveled out this way. I thought if I drove up here and saw for myself, I'd get a feeling."

"A feeling?"

"Whether she'd been here. Whether she was . . ."

"Still here?" he asked quietly.

I didn't answer. It started to snow. My heart sped up a bit. Being from Victoria, I felt awe and a vague panic. I said as much to Cobain as we drove.

"Ha," he said, thumping the steering wheel. There was a line of dirt under the half-moons of his nails, possibly from working on the turtle enclosure. "That's just what it's like falling in love, Nico, panic and awe. You'll see, one day." He smiled, pleased again. I smiled, too, happy at his faith in me. One day, I would fall in love.

"Why, in the name of all that is holy, are there no coffee shops along here?" he asked.

It was because there was cliff face on one side of the highway and an expanse of ocean on the other, but I decided to stay silent. Cobain was eccentric. He was an artist, after all.

"Wait until you see the Chief. It's where all the climbers go. It's a mondo granite monolith. Peregrine falcons nest there, too," Cobain said, sounding as excited as a little kid.

"I didn't know you liked nature so much."

"I appreciate the epic, Nico. Go big or go home. And the Squamish Chief is epic."

"It's the Stawamus Chief, actually. Named after a First Nation. Someday I want to climb it. Once I learn to rock climb." I hadn't told many people I wanted to learn to climb, just Obe.

"Really?" He looked at me, hair flopping over one eye. "A daredevil, eh?" He sped up the car to goad me, not such a good idea with the traffic and the snow pelting down. I said nothing. Highway 99 made me feel like a fruit fly. It looked as if the gods had gotten in a mad frenzy and thrown boulders around. Everything was big and blue or covered in snow. I had never seen anything like it. I only hoped the rock face would hold up and not sweep us to our deaths. I hadn't noticed any chains in the trunk of the Phoenix. We were poorly prepared for winter conditions.

"Well, you're only what, sixteen? There's still time."

"I'm fifteen," I said. "Born December 3, 1991. Conceived March 9, 1991. Or maybe March 8."

"How can you know that?" he laughed, then frowned, looking down the road.

"Do you—" I began, then changed my mind.

"Do I what?"

"Do you have regrets?" I was thinking a lot about things that can't be undone. I didn't want Verne to hate me.

"Oh yeah, of course."

"The biggest?"

"Leaving my daughter," he said immediately, as if answering a quiz question. "Because that changed everything."

A driver in a gray minivan honked as Cobain veered slightly out of his lane. The vehicles around us were crammed with people wearing colorful parkas, their skis secured in tidy racks. They could likely afford season ski passes and regular upgrades to equipment. As far as gear, I'd only ever had one proper backpack, that was it, and it was gone.

"Can we put on a CD?" I asked, to stop myself from thinking about the missing albums.

"I'm guessing you might like Sonic Youth," he said, gesturing to the stack of CDs wedged in the space behind the parking brake. The CD player in the car looked like a garage-sale reject, but it seemed to work.

"How did you know?" I hadn't mentioned Sonic Youth.

He turned toward Howe Sound for a moment. Snow was blowing across the black-blue water and swirling on the highway. It seemed unlikely Cobain's Pontiac Phoenix would have snow tires.

"I saw your T-shirt, the vintage one."

"The one that was in my pack, wrapped carefully around my CDs, and part of my private belongings?"

"Yes."

"What the hell?"

"I needed to look for drugs, Nico. I don't know you. I couldn't have you around if you had drugs, okay? I just couldn't. Sorry." Fat flakes socked against the windshield, and the wipers groaned over and over.

"And one other thing," he said, hunched over the wheel. The man had the posture of a garden hose.

"What?" I wasn't actually that angry. The farther we drove up the highway, the closer I was getting to my answer. I could feel it.

"I kept some of the CDs. I hadn't heard the albums for a

long time, so I wanted to give them a listen. You had some good ones. I was always planning to give them back."

"You stole them?" I felt tears prick my eyes, but strangely, I laughed. He had saved the CDs.

"Technically, yes."

"I love you, Cobain," I said, but I couldn't hear my words. I was drowned out by the sound of angry sirens, like screaming bees swarming around us.

Cobain did not pull over, despite the sirens. His instinct was to evade, to run, so instead he yanked the car off the highway at Porteau Cove Provincial Park. There was to be no fiery chase for us, unless we drove into the ocean. He parked. I looked at the water and the trees scoured clean by winter. They stood in a line like witches' brooms. The park was known as a place to scuba dive in the summer. We could plunge into the frigid water together, but we would not surface. I thought of the chorus to "Dive." Would he pick me? That was what I had done my whole life: waited for someone to choose me. I stepped out of the car, and the wind whipped my blue hair across my face. I needed showering, and flossing, and laundering.

Cobain got out, too. We had lost the cops. They hadn't expected we would bolt.

"I think she was here. She loved being outside, you know. She didn't like being confined," I told Cobain. My eyes filled with tears while snow coated my face. The mountains went blurry. She didn't like me, I was saying. I don't think my mother liked me.

"Nico, I'm not good at these things, but you're going to be okay. You just have to wait this out. And if you were . . ."

I tried to picture what Porteau Cove would be like in the summer, when it was a popular place to camp. I imagined families unpacking their tents and bags of jumbo marsh-mallows and beach towels. There were rail tracks nearby, where the Rocky Mountaineer would chug past. There was nothing more indifferent than a train.

The sirens were getting closer. I could tell Cobain was scared, because suddenly he became calm and still.

"Nico, I . . . I need to apologize. I'm not really the best grown-up. I wasn't a good dad, or husband, for that matter. . . ."

"THIS IS THE POLICE. STEP AWAY FROM THE CAR. GET DOWN ON THE GROUND AND PUT YOUR HANDS ON YOUR HEAD. NOW."

Cobain looked around. There were three police cars and more sirens in the distance. I turned to face the water, getting one last glimpse. *Where are you?* I wondered. She had been here. I knew that. Had she drowned, or fallen through ice? Or had she been taken?

Then all these cops had their guns drawn on Cobain. The pulsing lights circled around me. Cobain was on the ground, being handcuffed. I had done this.

"Leave him alone!" I tried to shout. Arms were around me, too. I punched at the body that held me, but it was solid, strong. I heard that I was safe now. Noise, and uniforms, and sirens, and snow. The famous Royal Canadian Mounted Police. If they were so great, how come they couldn't find my mother? I did not want to be apart from Cobain. But I never got what I wanted.

"I'm sorry," I sobbed as they took Cobain. "I'm sorry!"

I saw him turn to me, a flash from those blue eyes. Not "Help me, Nico," or "You hurt me, Nico," but just, "I tried, Nico." As they led him away, he straightened to his full height. He was taller than I had thought.

They asked if I was hurt. Not like they meant, no. Did I need a hospital, a doctor, a social worker, a therapist? Had he touched me? No, no, no, no. I would be sent home, back to Vancouver Island, this time commencing with a long ride in a police car. Did I want a juice or a tea?

Coffee. Please.

"When can I see him again?" I asked, when I finally managed to produce a full sentence.

"Your dad will be at the station. We've told him that we found you."

"I want to see Cobain. When can I see Cobain?"

"I don't know who you mean, honey." This was from a female cop with teak-brown hair. Power bangs, like an awning above her face.

I realized it was best to shut up. I had so many more questions for Cobain. I had wanted to hear him sing, if only once. I watched the scenery flash by, as if this were my montage in a movie. No one seemed to believe that they had actually found me. They seemed to think it had been too easy.

"Where are they taking him?'

"Who?"

"The man I was with." I thought about the kind of people who had sat in the same cop car, looking out the same window: murderers, drug dealers, and molesters. And me.

"Don't worry about him. We're going to make sure you get back home with your dad."

I hugged myself. I stayed quiet. Inside I wailed, wanting Cobain.

CHAPTER 15

"ALL APOLOGIES"

My mistake had been jumping out at Horseshoe Bay. Not surprisingly, I had been seen. At the RCMP station in West Vancouver, I answered the same questions over and over. No, Cobain had not hurt me. He had not touched me. I was not on drugs or alcohol. Verne had not hurt me. I had just gone away for a few days, to think. Wasn't that what people did?

"I want to speak with Detective Stanton at the Victoria Police," I said. "I need to talk to him about my mother."

The sergeant, Horvath, seemed unsatisfied with my answers about Cobain, or O'Ryan, as they called him. If I told the Mounties what they wanted to hear, would they search for my mother again? If I said Cobain had kidnapped me, held me against my will, would they do what I wanted? I considered it for one shameful moment. The truth: If I hadn't met Cobain, I might have gone crazy, succumbed. Given in to my pack of white wolves.

Horvath's nose was too big for his face. His face was thin, but his nose was a monster home on a small lot. Underneath it was the stereotypical cop mustache. I focused on that. I was one baby step away from crying. They would not tell me where they'd sent Cobain.

"You're in quite a bit of trouble, young lady. You don't seem to realize that," Horvath said. "Can you tell me again how you wound up in Vancouver?"

I sighed. The interview room smelled of the same lemon floor cleaner as Cobain's cabin, which stopped me for a second. Horvath stood in front of me, and some social worker was sitting in the corner. She had a straight part down her scalp, showing her chalk-white skin. The woman, Maria, wore a beige wool sweater and a beige wool skirt and held a notebook and a file. She seemed afraid of me. I was afraid of the file. I tried to explain about the homeless man again, the cold night in the ferry terminal.

"Why did you feel you needed to leave, Nicola? Maybe you weren't getting enough attention? Wanted to be in the papers?" asked Horvath.

"Only one person called me Nicola," I snapped, jerking forward. "You can call me Ms. Cavan, or Nico." I fell back in the plastic chair, surprised at my own words. "Horvath," I said, forgetting his title again. "Mr. Horvath. Please. I have new information. I think my mother was heading to Whistler when she disappeared, trying to see her friend who was working there. Can you get someone to recheck the files or something? Your officers can talk to my mother's friend, Janey Keogh. She lives in North Vancouver."

"What hold does that fellow have on you?" asked Horvath, leaning in. He smelled of stale coffee, an odor I detested. Fresh coffee was the smell of possibility. Stale coffee was a Greyhound bus ride.

"Please tell Stanton. He said he cared. He said he still thought about her," I sobbed.

"I think she's had enough for now, Staff Sergeant Horvath," the beige lady said, looking up from a handheld device. "Her father just arrived. She's answered all of your questions."

I had never seen a Mountie up close before: the crisp shirt, the badges, the lapels like arrows. His black cap had a bright gold band with a badge in the middle. I was afraid of him, which I figured was what he wanted. Did they even usually wear the hats? My greatest fear, however, was that he wouldn't listen to me.

"Ms. Cavan, did you know that girls, women, are disappearing from downtown Vancouver and we don't know why? And when we hear that a girl, a young woman, has gone missing . . . Do you know what you've put your father through? I have a daughter your age."

"You wouldn't want her to be friends with me, I guess," I said quietly. All the cops had a daughter my age, it seemed.

"That's not what I was saying, and I think you know that. We'll take you to your father now. He flew over by floatplane to get you."

My thoughts were scrambled, and I forgot that he meant

Verne, not Cobain. Horvath surveyed me again, as if uncertain I was worth the expense of a floatplane. "If what you say is true, you're lucky all you lost was a backpack."

When he was still nobody, like me, Kurt Cobain was arrested for spraying graffiti. After becoming famous, he later observed that one good thing about jail would be not signing autographs. "If it's illegal to rock and roll, throw my ass in jail," Kurt Cobain said. He also hoped he died before he became Pete Townshend, the guitarist from the Who.

I tried not to think of all the bad things I'd read about Cobain, such as the times he was supposedly too strung out to see his baby daughter, or didn't bother to thank people who needed thanking, or when he was childish and selfish and had poor hygiene. He was a genius. He had a problem with drugs. So what. Everyone's got something, I figured. Some of the biographers had described him doing things that were just *crazy*, but that's how those people sell books, right? Making up stories about people who can't defend themselves. I didn't believe most of it. Kurt Cobain wrote one of the best rock albums of all time; who wouldn't be jealous?

I wondered how I could see Cobain again. Would he go back to the cabin? Where was the cabin? I wasn't sure I could find it again. The social worker, Maria, led me through a set of glass security doors, and then I was looking up into the face of Verne. I nearly gasped. He seemed to have aged five years for every day I'd been gone. His eyes were pinched and red, as if he'd been crying or rubbing them. His rosacea had flared up, but he was clean-shaven, a task he sometimes neglected if I wasn't there to remind him. When he saw my face, his gray eyes lit up for a second, and then he clasped me in a hug, crushing me against his raincoat. He'd worn his good London Fog, which was reserved for important occasions.

"Verne, I . . ." I couldn't think of a thing to say. I was sorry.

We took the bus to the terminal and rolled onto the bowels of the boat, my third ferry in less than forty-eight hours. The driver parked the bus and shouted instructions for reboarding later, and Verne and I walked up to the passenger decks in silence. If we had spoken, something would have shattered. I realized I was glad to be going home, where there would be a hot shower. Verne seemed to relax once we were on the ferry to Victoria, the adrenaline easing off. I didn't want to think about what the floatplane had cost.

"Do you want a Nanaimo bar or anything?" he asked. All around us, people were staking out their areas with shopping bags full of their Christmas loot. How important it was for human beings to claim their little parcel of territory, even for a ninety-minute voyage. *I am here. This is mine. Keep off.*

"What?" I asked, my mind still running over the cabin, Highway 99, seeing Cobain down on the ground.

"You used to love them when you were little," Verne said. He had sagged into a seat by the window and was fixated on the black water instead of looking at me.

"Did I?" I didn't remember that. "They gave me a sandwich at the station. I'm okay."

He winced, as if not wanting to remember that his daughter had just been at a police station.

"Gillian has been sick with worry. So have I. We tried to keep it from Grandma Irene, but then it was all over the news."

"I know. I'm sorry." I was always sorry.

"What were you thinking, Nico?"

"I thought I could help find her." An elderly couple behind us was having a loud and tedious discussion about the need to have an electric garage door repaired. The faulty door seemed to take on the tenor of a tsunami or killer bees. "It's going to cost a pretty penny," the old man kept saying, a term I hadn't heard outside of movies. *Pretty penny.*

"Nico, that was so dangerous. I don't know where to start. That man who picked you up. He could have . . . What if he . . ." Verne was about to cry.

"He didn't. I'm fine. Verne, I think she was going to Whistler, to see Janey. I have a feeling. I went to talk with Janey when I was in Vancouver."

"You found her?"

I felt a flicker of pride then, chased by shame. Cobain had found her, not me. Or rather, Cobain's Nanaimo connection had found her.

"Yes, I did. She said you didn't want her to see me, Verne. My mother's best friend."

"It was a confusing time, Nico. You were so little. I just

wanted to protect you. The woman I loved was gone." He kept gazing at the shadowy water. The elderly couple jabbered about a son-in-law the old man hated.

"Janey said I needed to talk to you. That there were things you weren't telling me. You need to tell me now, Verne." I was dirty and tired and every muscle in my body ached. The man who had once defended me from my nightmares had betrayed me. "You need to tell me the truth. Did you even love her? Did you even love my mother? You always just go around like some robot!" I shouted. The old people stopped talking.

"Nico, I did love your mother. I loved her more than anything except you."

"Then why didn't you—"

"The truth is that Annalee didn't love me. Or she didn't love me anymore. She wanted to move to the mainland."

"What?" I felt as if my seat were rocking.

"I guess I'm not that good at loving people, Nico. I suppose I take after my dad. Annalee wanted to get away."

"From me."

"No, not you. She wanted to take you with her."

"You were going to get a divorce?"

"Nico." He sighed and rubbed his eyes. "We were never married."

"But I saw the photos: Mom in the white dress at Grandma Irene's place in Kelowna. You had strawberries on your wedding cake. Mom had flowers in her hair."

"That was just a family party for you and for her. When we found out you were on the way. You were a surprise.

Then you surprised us again when you arrived a month early."

"Why did you lie? No one cares about that these days."

"I wanted to marry her, Nico. But she didn't love me enough. She had a lot of passions: her music, the mountains. She wasn't a make-do kind of person. She was quiet but intense, kind of like you."

I felt a chill, the way you do when you realize someone has been watching you after all, that they *know* you.

"She had no living relatives of her own, you know that, so I think she was drawn to someone dependable, like me. I guess dependable only gets you so far. I had been planning to go to the police academy before you were born, but then that was put on hold."

On hold, like, forever. Verne had wanted to be a cop?

"Verne," I started. There didn't seem to be anything left to say. My parents had never even been married. Annalee had wanted out. But she had wanted me.

"I didn't want her to take you away from me, Nico. You know that, right? I wouldn't have let that happen."

"I just really miss her," I said, and then I couldn't stop crying. I made this high-pitched noise, like keening, I guess. I ran to the washroom, bumping into a lady towing her toddler along for a walk. The mother glared at me. I ran into a stall and clicked the metal door shut. I sat down on the toilet and sobbed for a long time. Long enough that Verne sent a white-haired woman in an orange fleece vest to ask if I was okay. Long enough that an announcement came on: "Ladies and gentlemen, we are now approaching the Swartz Bay ferry terminal. We ask that you please return to your vehicles." That meant I had two choices: find my way back to the bus parked in the bowels of the ferry, or hide in the cubicle until a cleaner walked in and called security.

I'd had enough of ferries. I bumped out of the stall and washed my hands, barely recognizing the girl in the mirror with the gray skin and the now-blue-tinged hair. I looked as if I needed vegetables, antioxidants, and exfoliation. Verne had done what I asked and was nowhere to be seen. Or maybe I'd finally crossed the line and he'd given up on me. The passenger lounges were now almost empty except for the uniformed workers bustling around. A lady in a white uniform and a big perm like a forsythia bush glared at me. I had a wonky sense of direction at the best of times. It would be a miracle if I found the bus.

I flew down the concrete stairs, afraid I was going to do a face-plant. I'd never noticed how much a ferry is like a prison, with all the metal doors slamming shut. Engines were revving. I had left it too late. The lower vehicle level was like an underwater cave, and the cars and trucks seemed like snarling animals with their red and yellow eyes. I couldn't remember which end the buses parked in. It was as if I had been spun in one of those children's party games and left to stumble around blindfolded. Then I heard Verne: "Nico, this way."

He stood by the open bus door making sweeping Xs in the air with his long arms. As the cars started up around me, I ran, my legs scraping the sides of cars. I pounded up the steps and the bus driver shut the door.

"Look who decided to join us," the driver barked. The ferry ramp clanked down like a drawbridge, and we rumbled out into the night.

CHAPTER 16

"SLIVER"

It felt strange to be back in my room. It looked small and, well, messy. Had I left it that way, or had the police searched it? I was glad, and maybe surprised, that Verne had been so intent on finding me. I could hear him out in the hall explaining the night's events to my aunt. Gillian had been, Verne told me, "almost hysterical" when she found out I was missing. It was hard to picture. I knew Gillian would be hurt and angry, and that part stung. She had always stood by me, no matter what.

Obe had been emailing: *Where R U?* Verne had called him in Winnipeg, asking if he knew where I was. Obe was still visiting his grandparents but would be back for New Year's, just before school started again. School. I had not imagined going back to Vic High, ever. I had only been gone two days in Seattle and three days with Cobain, but my room seemed foreign. It was like going back to kinder-garten and seeing how tiny all the easels and desks really were all along. Still, I swept the clothes and CDs off the bed, lay down, and closed my eyes. Let the Frog Man come. I was too tired to care.

$$\mathscr{N}$$

When I woke up, it took a few seconds to cut through the netting of my dreams and remember where I was. I could hear Verne bustling around in the kitchen. His Christmas tree, the one he had been so excited about, leaned against a wall. Its base was stuck in an empty tin can full of water to keep the needles fresh, which struck me as hopeful, as if he thought I'd be back. It was still undecorated. It was just a pine tree in the living room.

"Thanks, Verne," I said when I sat down at the kitchen table. The sun filtered through the window in a way that reminded me of party streamers. No one had made me food since Cobain had prepared me the mac and cheese. I was desperate to hear news of Cobain, but I couldn't let Verne know how much I cared. I had already asked him twice what had happened to the man who gave me a ride. Verne didn't know. But I also had another pressing issue: there were only a few days before school resumed. I had to make my point clear.

"Verne, I was serious. She was heading to Whistler to see Janey. We need to make the police understand."

I couldn't see his face, because I was sitting and he was frying pancakes and veggie sausages, both for me.

"Nico, you realize that they checked everywhere for her. Everywhere." He looked down while he squirted some syrup on the pancakes. It was Aunt Jemima. Our budget did not extend to real maple syrup. Still, the pancakes were just what I wanted. I ate four, a record for me. Then I had a hot shower, soaping myself down twice. The police had still not found my backpack. I also didn't know how I would find Cobain. I could track down Jasper Jameson's publicist, but I would seem like a crazy fan, the type he was hiding from. I would wait.

The idea of going back to school was surreal. Obe would be home in two days. He had no idea of all that had happened to me. I felt bad that the holidays were almost over. Some Christmas for Verne.

"Verne," I said. "Do you want to decorate your tree? It could be for New Year's."

He took me up on my invitation and we hung a few things on the tree. There were old decorations I had made in elementary school and a couple that were from my mother's family: a girl elf and a china figure of Father Christmas, looking proper and British, as was my mother's family.

I was sitting in the living room, enjoying being full and clean and wondering if and when I was going to face the music for what I'd done, when the phone rang. I figured it was Gillian or Grandma Irene, but I could hear Verne sounding stern, speaking with a forced politeness.

"And that's all I have to say," he said, and the phone clicked back into the receiver.

"Who was—" The doorbell cut me off. It made an old-fashioned bird-in-distress sound rather than a more melodious modern tone.

Verne came rushing in, flushed. "I'll get it," he said, still holding a tea towel from drying the dishes. I should have offered to help, I realized. I was feeling vacant, hollowed out.

"May I help you?" Verne asked. I got up off the couch and walked toward the door. Visitors were unusual.

There was a lady standing on the porch. She had blond hair, flat-ironed and satiny, and wore a teal raincoat. She gripped a tape recorder. There was a man positioned at the end of the drive, holding a TV camera hoisted on his shoulder. I heard her say her name, Tina something.

Through the window I could see a white van with *Channel 6* written on the side parked in the street.

"No," I heard Verne say. "We're just glad she's home and well."

I wanted to get a better look, but Verne waved me back.

"I can't comment on that, either," he said. "The police issued a press release. You can ask them any questions."

The police issued a press release? I watched the cameraman through the window. He hadn't seen me, but he was filming. Just then a car pulled up. The logo of the daily newspaper was stenciled on the side. A man and a woman hopped out and also scurried up the drive. I remembered that Sean wanted to be a journalist.

"Nico," Verne hissed from the side of his mouth. "Please go to your room."

I did, mostly because Verne rarely gave direct orders,

and I was a little stunned. I sat on the bed, waiting. I had never done anything of any importance before. Except for my missing mother, I had always been unremarkable. Was I kidding myself about Sean?

He had sent me an email, though, albeit a brief one. *Hey, R U home? What are u doing for New Year's? Might go to a show at the uni . . . Write me. I miss Y, Sean.* The message sent me into a tizzy. Surely he had meant "U" instead of "Y." Because who was "Y"? Or did it stand for something? The two letters were right beside each other on the keyboard.

I hadn't written back yet. I wasn't sure what to tell him about the past few days. Cobain. The cabin. Cobain. My night at the ferry terminal, my talk with Janey: everything, endless and nameless.

I heard Verne say something loud and emphatic and then shut the door. A pause. I heard him lock it. That sent a wriggle of chills down my shoulder blades.

"What did they want?" I asked when he came and stood in the doorway.

"They wanted you to go on camera, or barring that, me. They heard about the mystery man you were found with. The story is in today's papers."

We didn't get the newspaper. Verne liked radio or TV, and I wasn't overly concerned with current affairs. I didn't much care for news of the real world. I liked music and art.

"I guess you can talk to them if you want to, but I wanted to let you get some rest first. You didn't look too good last night." He frowned. He was still holding the tea towel. It was the cheap kind bought at the grocery store in packs of three. "Hopefully, tomorrow they'll move on to another story and we can go on with our lives." He studied the Christmas tree, thinking. "They were asking questions about Annalee, too. This whole mess has gotten the reporters talking about the case again. They probably think I'm some kind of monster, driving people away," he said, sounding deflated.

I heard a vehicle rumbling outside again, but it was just one of the green linen-supply trucks. I hoped our neighbors hadn't seen the cameras, especially the old lady who lived downstairs. She hardly ever spoke to us, but she watched. She rarely left her suite, except to sweep her front steps or to sit in a cast-iron lawn chair to survey the street. When I was little, she apparently complained to the landlord about the noise my feet made scampering above her. She seemed bitter about everything, as if life had passed her by.

"Verne," I said. "I'd like to talk to the reporters."

"Nico, are you sure?" He looked as if he regretted telling me it was my choice. He hadn't expected me to make that one.

"I want it to be a big story," I said. "I'll tell them everything."

Almost everything.

CHAPTER 17

"PENNYROYAL TEA"

I owned only one pair of good dress shoes: black Mary Janes. Getting ready that morning, I used about half a bottle of apricot-scented shampoo, lathering and rinsing, lathering and rinsing. The washing made my hair dull but turned down the blue a notch or two. I wore a denim skirt and a violet blouse with ties down the front that Grandma Irene had given me last year along with the Mary Janes. My tights had a hole in the heel, but it wouldn't show. The press conference was at the police station on Caledonia Avenue, just a short walk from our place. Verne and I were awkward around each other, as if getting acquainted again. Perhaps he had imagined life without me and hadn't liked the idea. In turn, I now appreciated his life skills, such as having more than I Can't Believe It's Not Butter in the fridge.

Verne touched my shoulder as we sat down behind a long table. There were so many lights beating down. He tucked a strand of hair behind my ear and gestured to the microphones in front us. "Should I do my karaoke version of 'Light My Fire'?" he asked with a weak smile. I smiled back.

There were two TV cameras positioned on either side of the table and four reporters sitting in the rows of chairs facing us. They had handheld tape recorders and clutched spiral notepads. It wasn't a big crowd, but of course, it wasn't a big story. I was just another missing teenager who had been found.

It was time for me to speak, probably the closest I would ever come to giving a performance. I know what I said to them, because I read from a page torn from my sketch-book.

"I want to thank all the police officers from Victoria and the Lower Mainland who assisted me in returning home safely. Now I ask the public's help in finding my mother, Annalee Lester."

(I had written *HOLD UP PHOTO*.)

"As some of you have already reported, my mother went missing almost eleven years ago, in February of 1996. I am asking the public to think again if you saw her then or you know where she is now. Imagine what it is like to have no answers when someone you love goes missing, when they disappear and never return."

(I had written *HOLD UP PHOTO AGAIN*.)

And that was the end of my speech. The rest was a blur

of reporters standing up and sitting down, and someone asked about the man I was with when I was found—a passing motorist had snapped a blurry photo of him—and the room fell silent. I swear I could hear the tape recorders whirring, like bees in a hive. Even the police spokeswoman appeared interested in my response. Verne, next to me, seemed to stop breathing, his broad shoulders hitched forward.

"He was no one. He was just someone who gave me a ride. I was trying to find my mother," I said.

The police representative shut down the questions with a decisive "That's it, ladies and gentlemen," and led us out a back door. Then Verne and I walked home together in a light, cold rain. We said nothing, just walked. Halfway home, we stopped to wait for a red light and Verne held out his hand. I hesitated, and then took it.

"Your mother always had cold hands, too," said Verne.

I tried to remember the last time he had taken my hand. "Did you really want to be a police officer?"

"Yes," he said as we turned up our street. A man wearing an orange safety vest lugging yellow plastic bags from the dollar store gave me a funny look. I remembered that my photo had been everywhere, in the newspapers and on TV. Missing. I was the girl who went missing, a distinction I now shared with my mother. The house was freezing when we got home, so I cranked up the heat. I had an email tagged urgent from Obe. *NICO: WTF?* was the subject line. Then a single line in the body: *Are you okay? Worried here.*

I wrote back: *Yes, okay. Long story. I think I met my real father. You won't believe who he is.* I was about to hit send; then I couldn't, because something was bothering me. When the cops had Cobain surrounded, when he got out of that car, when Cobain was raised to his full height—he was too tall. He was simply too tall. I had tried to forget about it all the way home, the whole ferry ride, and then again when the reporters asked about the mystery man. Cobain, with his hands clamped on his head and those beautiful eyes sparking with panic, had looked tall, too tall.

So I just wrote *Yes, okay. Long story. Went to see my mother's friend.*

Then I finally wrote back to Sean: *Home again, thanks. And thanks for showing me around. Don't know about New Year's yet. Probably see what my friend Obe is doing.* Then I couldn't decide how to sign it. *Hugs?* Too girlie. I considered *xoxo*, but that meant hugs and kisses, right? Sean didn't seem to be an *xoxo* kind of guy. It would be strange to tell Obe about him. It had always been the two of us.

I hadn't faced any of the real-life frog men chasing me—my brain had been too busy—but sitting in my room reminded me of all those things. The missing CDs. How everyone at school hated me, and that big moron, Liam, who had called me a dog. I hadn't thought about any of those miseries while I was on the road with Cobain, or whoever he was.

Verne watched the TV news just before dinnertime. I said I didn't want to see it. I didn't want to see me. Then Verne made quesadillas and salad.

"I thought you looked a lot like her, when I saw you on TV," he said, chewing a piece of lettuce.

My hair was now like skim milk, blond-white with a blue tinge.

"Can you tell me something about her?"

"Well," he said. "You know she liked the outdoors. Her parents were quite the hikers, too; that's partly why they immigrated to this part of the country."

I vaguely remembered seeing a thick green sleeping bag that was said to belong to my mother's father. I wondered where it had been stored.

"She liked to sing to you. Sometimes nursery rhymes, or folk songs, or some of the rock music she liked."

"I remember her singing 'Seasons in the Sun,'" I said.

"She called you Little Early because you were little."

"And I woke up early."

"No, actually, it was because you arrived early. We didn't even have a crib yet."

"Why couldn't you tell me about her?"

"It was too hard, Nico. I hoped they would find her. I really thought they would find her. Then I didn't want you to know that—"

"That what?"

"That she was going to leave me. I wanted you to think we were happy." He said this in a flat tone, as if he'd rehearsed it so many times that saying it was as simple as a sigh. "I wanted you to believe we were a happy family."

"Maybe we were," I said, wanting to believe it too.

Verne half smiled. Verne was usually too hesitant to give life a whole smile. One biographer of Kurt Cobain said few photographs in existence captured how wide his smile could be. You could see it in his childhood photos, a joyous grin from ear to ear; then something happened. Or maybe the people taking the pictures wanted something different. Certainly no rock photographers would ask Kurt Cobain, guitar deity and lead singer of Nirvana, to beam as if someone had just promised him Dairy Queen and a free puppy.

My mother always smiled with her lips closed, though I am told she had white, straight teeth. Had she been happy when she left me that day when I was four? If she had been happy, why did she leave? It made no sense. I needed Obe back home to listen, though he was probably tired of hearing about my problems. He had his own issues. If we ever used the Ouija board again, I thought, I would ask more about Obe's future. Except I knew we would never use the board again. Things were different. I was done with that.

I opened up my scratched secondhand laptop. I was glad it hadn't been in the stolen backpack. I searched *John Simon Ritchie*, the name on the pill bottles. Turned out he was better known as Sid Vicious, that guy from the Sex Pistols. He died in 1979, so some doctor was being conned. Then I tried Jasper Jameson. The third suggested search term was *Jasper Jameson net worth*, so I tried that. The answer was $5.5 million. Apparently writing thrillers could be lucrative. Then I searched *Daniel O'Ryan+Seattle*. The search produced hundreds of hits, among them a publishing blog suggesting it was the real name of Jasper Jameson, bestselling author. Jameson, an eccentric, had chosen to stay out of the public eye despite creating seven bestselling thrillers published in thirty-two countries, three optioned for film. Hometown: Tacoma, Washington. Age: forty. Was once a high school teacher. Upcoming book: untitled, publication fall 2007. He was notorious for looking disheveled and poor, even though he was supposedly loaded. In 2004, there were rumors that he turned up at the Sundance Film Festival, where a movie based on one of his books was premiering. "That's Jasper Jameson?" one festivalgoer is reported as saying. "He looks like a wino."

The site had a caveat suggesting that the bio was incomplete, and anyone with more information should write in. I tried another search of *Jasper Jameson*. I clicked on a celebrity gossip site: *Jasper Jameson's real identity has been fraught with mystery and speculation. He is said to retreat to isolated rural areas to write free from the public eye.*

It was confusing, all these aliases. Then there were the names on the prescription meds. It seemed just as well that Cobain wasn't a high school teacher anymore. Still, I wanted to see him again. He was the first adult who was not a relative who had known me for me and liked me, besides Obe's mom. I wondered if Detective Stanton would tell me where Cobain had gone. I only knew that the police had let him go. I had told them . . . well, nothing. I had said he had given me a ride, and that he'd been kind, and nothing had happened. How could I tell Stanton that I wanted to see him, Cobain/Jameson/O'Ryan? Could I say I wanted to thank him? That might get Cobain in trouble. I did not want that. He had done enough.

Obe, needless to say, was pissed at me when he heard the whole story, or most of it. He had an accordion file of grievances. I had not communicated with him about meeting Sean; running away; sleeping rough; hanging out in a cabin near Nanaimo with, in his words, "a psycho in a Pontiac Phoenix"; or finding Janey and Ange. I filled him in on all these things while we sat cross-legged in my living room, he nursing an instant coffee, me with a strawberry Quik. I did not mention the name Kurt Cobain to Obe. I figured you have to keep some things to yourself, like kindling inside for when you need it. I told Obe only that the man I met on the ferry was an artist and a writer and that no one else knew about my stay with him.

"Obe, you have to promise not to tell anyone about the cabin. They'll go after him. It could be life or death," I added. "Swear on the name of that girl at school you like. What's her name?" I felt as if we had been apart for months.

"I don't like her anymore," he said swiftly. "I met a girl in Winnipeg. Kimber." Obe looked wistful at the mention of her name. "We met at a party I went to with my cousin. We . . ." He paused for dramatic effect. "Hit it off."

"Obe!" I shrieked. "You didn't!"

"No, or yes, depending on what you're asking. I'm going back at March break to see my grandparents again." Obe had a smile on his face as wide as a fruit bowl.

"Does she like good music?" I asked, feeling a slight rustle in my gut. I wasn't sure I wanted to share Obe.

"I'm helping her with that," he said, not meeting my eyes.

"That's great, Obe," I said. "I'd like to meet her."

"Thanks, Nico. It might not work out, but I'd rather just enjoy this feeling for a while and not worry about it."

I gave him a hug, quickly, just around the shoulders. I loved Obe, but I had trouble telling him so. The hug surprised him, and he smiled his sweet, lopsided smile.

"Okay, well, so, let's listen to some music. I got an album by Winnipeg's own the Weakerthans while I was away. It is totally, utterly awesome," he said. "Want to hear?"

Yes.

CHAPTER 18

"YOU KNOW YOU'RE RIGHT"

A lot of people call Nirvana a Seattle band, but that's not where they began. Kris and Kurt were about my age when they started a band, and that was in Aberdeen. Then they both lived in Olympia. Seattle was later. It was, however, where the body of Kurt Cobain was reportedly found. It was discovered April 8, 1994, in the greenhouse above the garage of his Lake Washington mansion, which he shared with his wife and baby, a nanny or two, and some drug dealers and junkies who came and went. In the days before, Kurt Cobain had jumped the wall of a drug rehab center in California and gotten on a plane back to Seattle. His wife had frozen his credit cards. At the airport, he signed autographs for a few fans. Courtney Love was in Los Angeles but hired a private investigator to search Seattle for her husband.

According to media reports, there was a shotgun across his body. A note was found at the scene. There was a can of root beer and some heroin paraphernalia. His death was ruled suicide, but others suggested it was foul play. The circumstances of his death have been put under a microscope over and over, just like the deaths of John F. Kennedy, John Lennon, Princess Diana, and Jesus Christ. I read that Kurt Cobain went through a religious phase as a devout Christian while in high school. He later married Courtney Love in his pajamas on Waikiki Beach. That fact is better known.

An electrician named Gary Smith installing an alarm system on the property supposedly discovered Cobain's body. Upon hearing the news, someone from the electrician's company tipped off a local Seattle radio station, saying they'd better get some great concert tickets for that scoop.

Who wouldn't want to leave a world with that kind of heartless greed? It would be no wonder if Kurt Cobain opted out. If the man I met on the ferry was Kurt Cobain but had reinvented himself as Jasper Jameson, bestselling author, he was a millionaire recluse again, like it or not. And even if he was Jasper Jameson (but really Daniel O'Ryan, divorced former high school teacher), then he was still on the run from fame, from life. I might never see him again.

Nirvana's music showed a mastery of the soft/loud: a screeching chorus, grinding guitar, and then an interlude of quiet. *If you read you'll judge*, Kurt Cobain wrote on his journal. The diary was not meant for anyone to read. The art was what he left behind, the songs. Some accounts make Kurt Cobain sound deranged, an addict unable to care for himself, let alone a child. Or was he the musical genius of his time? He was a man who loved animals and children, his grandmother, a good joke. He supported feminism and gay rights and told homophobes and racists not to buy Nirvana albums. He was a cheerful, beloved child whose world was ripped apart by divorce. Maybe it's not fair to judge the dead. Gone is gone.

"I'm going away. But I'll be back before these flowers wilt," Annalee had told me. And I wonder, what if I had cried? I was only four, after all. What if I had thrown myself on the ground, or knocked over the flowers?

Would she have stayed?

Would she be alive?

Here I go, I could say into the black. The black could be soothing, like a moonless night over the ocean, or sad, like dilated pupils. It could be terrifying: the tar-colored gums of feral dogs. We don't know. I think about it, though. Oblivion. Kurt Cobain's cousin said she thought he was bipolar, which means you swing between being sad and happy. Maybe my aunt would say the same thing about me.

"Why didn't you tell me?" Gillian asked me over the phone. She was angry, most of all because she didn't think I kept secrets from her. But of course, I did. We all keep secrets. I hated hurting Gillian. I imagined her in her neat condo holding the phone, standing in her fit, wide-legged stance, always ready for anything.

"I didn't know. It was all last-minute. An impulse, I guess." *Runs in the family*, I thought, but did not say. "I'm sorry," I added.

"Oh, Nico," she sighed. I imagined her running her hand through that red hair. "I hope Verne will let you come see me again someday. You've put that all in jeopardy."

"I know." I just wanted her to forgive me. I needed her. "Maybe you could come visit us at Easter?" An offering.

"We'll see," she said. "I'm just glad you're not hurt." The last word came out as a sob. "I read about all those women going missing in Vancouver. I didn't know what to think. It made me glad I don't have children."

I waited. It was true that having children seemed to make people miserable, from everything I could gather, as did being married. *Buried.*

"I'm sorry, Nico. I didn't mean it that way."

"I know."

"It's not just children, it's caring about anyone. It leaves you vulnerable. I guess you could care about nobody, about nothing, and you'd never worry and never feel pain," she said. "I see a lot of people at the hospital looking for that."

"Yeah," I said. "It would be easier."

"Just promise me you won't do that again, run away. Call me and we'll run away together, okay?"

Okay, Gillian.

Kurt Cobain also had an aunt who loved him, Mari. She was a singer and helped him record at her home, both when he was a toddler and when he was older. She said that for Kurt, fame was like being sent into space without a spacesuit or spaceship. She and many other people loved him as best they could. He was not an abandoned man. That was not an excuse. If Kurt Cobain was dead, if he was really dead . . . The thought made me panic. The last song Nirvana ever recorded, "You Know You're Right," was released years after Cobain's death. In it, the singer promises not to bother you and not to follow. "Pain," he sings in the chorus, again and again, stretching out the word so the syllables form a landscape.

"Nico," I heard Verne saying. "Nico, I think we should sit and enjoy this Christmas tree. Otherwise a perfectly good pine died in vain."

"I'll be there in a minute," I said, cupping the receiver. "Wait for me."

CHAPTER 19

"WHERE DID YOU SLEEP LAST NIGHT?"

The first day of school reminded me of the scene from *The Wizard of* Oz, when the sinister trees come to life and snark at Dorothy for picking one of their apples. Clusters of students stood together in the hall, rooted, and when I passed them, head down, they would whisper: "That's the girl. That's the girl." But they wouldn't look my way. All the other kids seemed to be wearing brand-new clothes. One girl rocked a fancy purple fleece with the tag still sticking out behind the neck. Normally, that tag would have been ridiculed, but hey, Nico Cavan had run away to Vancouver and been hauled home by the cops.

I'd spent a quiet New Year's Eve with Obe, and on New Year's Day Verne assigned me various duties, including visiting Grandma Irene and helping with grocery shopping. Then I got to vacuum. Verne could be tough.

Going to school was not negotiable. I had nowhere to run, so I went.

Obe had shown up at my house at eight-thirty a.m., as was customary on school days, as if nothing had happened. Cold rain spat down. I had lost most of my favorite clothes with my backpack. Somewhere, a homeless man was walking around Vancouver in my vintage Sonic Youth T-shirt. I planned to keep that fact from Obe for as long as possible. I was learning how to keep secrets.

After school I trudged home, pining for my missing CDs. I felt as if something should happen. I'd been through so much, yet nothing had changed. On the corner there was a pile of four empty needle casings sticking straight up like blue weeds. Obe had gone off somewhere to play this game called *Guitar Hero*, which Sean also reported being hooked on. (*You must try it, Nico!* he wrote.) Apparently Obe now had another friend besides me, a guy from his French class.

The whole house still smelled of the vegetarian chili we'd eaten the night before. I sat on the carpet with my laptop and read the news articles about myself, even though I'd said I wouldn't. When a person goes missing, a lot happens at once. The police notify the bus lines, the ferries, the airports, and the taxi companies. They check bank accounts and look for credit-card transactions. They track cell phone use. It was amazing they hadn't caught me sooner.

One of the papers had a quote from Liam, that dim guy in grade 11. "'Nico always seemed kind of sad,' said Liam Tuck, 16, a student at Victoria High. 'I think she had a case of peer pressure.'"

Liam made peer pressure sound like a medical condition. The story said that when a person goes missing, the case boils down to one of four theories. They are presumed to have committed suicide, run away, been murdered, or had an accident. Of those four, I would choose to believe my mother ran away, because then she could still be alive. Alive and wanting nothing to do with me, obviously, but alive. Both she and I had escaped on ferries. I guess that's what happens when you live on an island.

I was tired. My bones ached. I put *In Utero* into my CD player and lay on my bed, letting the music drown out the crash of my thoughts. I listened to it once, then started again, when I heard a clatter at the door. I grabbed the baseball bat I kept in my closet. Then I heard a key turning. It was Verne.

"What's up?" I asked. "Thought you were on until eleven tonight." He'd been working split shifts lately.

"I booked off early. Thought we'd have dinner together. You do your homework. I'll heat up the chili and make a salad."

Then he walked into the kitchen. He might have made a good cop. He was level-headed and never acted on impulse. I used to be the same.

By the end of January, my blue hair was a memory and the dishwater blond was back. Obe continued to adore his mademoiselle in Winnipeg, and Gillian seemed to have forgiven me, even asking if I could come visit at Easter, perhaps with Verne. Sean had been emailing, just short messages about bands he'd seen or climbs he was planning to do. I checked my email for his messages more often than I cared to admit, smitten with the idea of him. I still had the photo of my mother and Kurt Cobain, and I glanced at it almost every night before bed, a kind of talisman, unless I fell asleep over my sketchbook.

Using an old childhood photo of Gillian and Verne, I made a painting of them as children, but with their older selves looming in the background. I gave it to Verne as a late Christmas present, and he liked it. In the real photo, he appeared sad, one arm around Gillian, who had her hair in two straight braids and was missing her front teeth. When I painted Verne as a child, I gave him a slight smile. It was the least I could do.

"Nico," he said, holding the painting in front of him like a cafeteria tray. "I'm no expert, but you could really have something."

Verne had started talking about trying to buy a town house in Vic West, maybe even a place close to the ocean instead of close to mattress outlets and linen supply depots. And I had done some paintings that I didn't hate. Some were pretty strange, so I kept those to myself.

A part of me the size of an eyelash dared to believe that my mother was still alive. The rest of me slammed down the gavel, insisting that she was dead or did not want to be found. Why had she gone? And worst of all, had she suffered, or was she suffering now?

I became used to my routine again. My sense of

adventure had dulled. I plodded along. Early in February I arrived home in the drizzle to find a piece of paper stuck on our door. I never expected good news. Were we being evicted? No, we weren't rich, but we weren't that poor.

It was a missed package delivery notice. Something for Ms. Nico Cavan. The notice had been left the day before, but it must have gone to the old lady downstairs. I turned around and headed to the post office, which was about fifteen minutes away. It was raining harder, but it didn't matter. I was going to get the package, whatever it was. Ms. Nico Cavan. It made me sound like a lawyer.

The post office downtown was overly spacious for the amount of business done there, and all the staff was cheerful.

"Package for you?" asked the clerk excitedly, as if I, or he, were five years old. He winked.

"Yes," I said, hoping he didn't recognize me from the news stories. I had been getting second glances, raised eyebrows. The white-paper package was about a foot long and padded with bubble wrap. I tucked it under my arm, resisting the urge to split it open like a fish right there in the post office. Was that a fairy tale? Something precious lost and then found in the belly of a fish? A ring? Or maybe it was an urban myth.

When I got home, I threw my knapsack on the floor, raced to the kitchen for a paring knife, and gutted the package. A piece of paper, neatly sliced in two by my knife, fluttered to the scuffed linoleum.

I tore through the bubble wrap like a surgeon trying to get to vital organs. Under the wrapping were my mother's CDs—all of them, it appeared. I made a sound, I think, a cry that was part happy, part surprise. I had the CDs back.

I put the two pieces of paper together and held them up.

Dear Nico,
  These belong to you. I hope these find you well, and home, and well.
  Your mother had good taste.
  Remember to be who you are, no matter what.
  Maybe we will see each other again, Nico. I hope so.
                    Peace and love,
                    Daniel

I crouched down and lined up the CDs on the floor tiles, which were the cheap press-and-stick kind, worn to a shade of dishrag gray. The bubble wrap reminded me of caterpillar cocoons. I sat on the floor, still in my jacket, and I cried. Because part of me had hoped it was a package from her. That she had finally sent word to me.

His words "be who you are" reminded me of how Cobain was always quoted as saying it's better to be hated for your real self than loved for being a phony. Could that be true? Could it be better to be hated? I blew my nose on a paper towel, found the phone book, and flopped it open. I dialed. I waited.

"May I speak with Detective Stanton, please?" I asked. "It's Nicola Cavan." I surprised myself by saying my full name.

I didn't even know if he was the man to help me. Both the Vancouver and the Victoria police had been involved in my mother's case, and mine, but the RCMP patrolled the Sea-to-Sky Highway, where I had been found. I didn't know the right thing to do. But I was done waiting. Stanton's voice mail snapped on, each word of his message as crisp as a September apple. I waited for the beep.

"This is Nicola Cavan. Detective Stanton, I'd really like to meet with you and talk about my mother, Annalee Lester. I was only four when she went missing, but now I'm older and I have a right . . . Can you just call me, please?"

I hung up. I wondered if my call would result in a visit from a social worker. Or maybe I had just sounded childish? No, I did have a right to know. I had a right to know.

Detective Stanton returned my call two days later with a perfunctory voice mail message left while I was at school. "Be assured, we are doing all we can, Ms. Cavan, and we will keep you informed of any developments on the case."

And so on. My phone call had been useless. Stanton might as well have patted me on the head. I stayed up most of that night fretting about my lack of progress and got up the next morning when it was still pitch dark. Verne had left early to drop the car off for repair. I hated winter. I hated everything. I walked to the front window and stared out into the street. It was 6:13 a.m. By the dim streetlights I could see there was a green-and-yellow bong left on the curb in front of our house the day before, and overnight someone had placed a bag of garbage next to it, right in our shitty front yard. A gray pickup truck I didn't recognize was parked across the street. The sky was oily gray, like fish scales.

What the hell? Was our front yard a dumping ground now? It was true what people said: garbage breeds more garbage, and one wall of graffiti soon becomes many, because not caring is contagious. There was an actual theory about it, with a name I couldn't remember.

Fuck it. I cared. I pulled on boots and marched out of the house in my pajamas and a fleece Obe had left behind. I hadn't had an email from Sean in a few days, and that pissed me off. I had no money to buy CDs, and that pissed me off. There was a nasty sheen of ice on the sidewalks, which also annoyed me.

I went to the curb, anger beaming from my body like a floodlight. I kicked the bong with my slipper, which killed my toe. I was going to hurl the bag of garbage, which seemed to be old clothes, when I noticed movement in my peripheral vision and whirled around to see a man sitting at the wheel of the truck. His eyes went wide, seeing my furious face. He turned and started the engine.

The truck was enormous, jacked up. It let out a single, forceful smoker's cough and roared to life.

"What the fuck do you want?" I screamed. "This is where I live. It's not a garbage dump." The man had a red knit cap, a mustache, a beard, and sunken eyes. He wore one of those puffy black jackets popular with gas station attendants. I leaned in closer to get a better look, ignoring all my years of warnings about how to stay safe in the streets. He had an ashtray full of Player's cigarettes, the white ones, and on the passenger side was a copy of the daily newspaper with me on the front page. Me: looking as if I were about to cry, despite how brave I tried to be. Me: holding up a photo of the beautiful Annalee.

"Do you know me?" I asked.

He gunned the engine, jerking the truck to the right on the sidewalk, since I blocked his escape, and forward, swinging around in a big U. The truck bumped around the narrow dead-end street. It was like watching a wounded bison thrashing.

"Come back!" I shouted as he lurched past. BUILT FORD TOUGH. I SUPPORT SQUAMISH SEARCH AND RESCUE, I read on his bumper. I tried to run but slipped on the ice, falling chest forward, the air punched out of me.

"Four two nine!" I yelled as I stood up. "Four two nine, you asshole!" It was the first three numbers of his license plate. It wasn't much.

My pajamas were covered in mud and grit. I brushed a cigarette butt from my thigh and limped across the street. The garbage bags appeared to have been stuffed with rags and random electronics that someone had given up on lugging around. Or perhaps they had been stolen and abandoned. There was also an old bowling trophy sitting on the curb that I hadn't noticed. There was something looped around the trophy, which was a single fake-gold pin on a black stand. *Sunrise Lanes, Third Place*, it read. I was afraid to touch the bracelet hanging off the trophy, but I did. I had to hold it right up to my face to see the red insignia, the snake squiggling around the staff, and the two words: *Medic* and *Alert*.

I don't remember going inside, but must have, because I found myself sitting on my bed still wearing my muddy slippers, running my finger over the lettering. On the other side, there was a 1-800 phone number and a medical ID number. In the middle were the words *Anaphylaxis: Allergic to bee stings*. Then I thought maybe I shouldn't have touched it, fingerprints and all, and dropped the chain on my bedspread.

After changing out of my pajamas, I called the police station and asked to speak to Stanton. It was still early, but I willed him to be there. "It's his daughter. I hit my head in practice and I need him to come pick me up!" I said, and then sniffled. "Oh please, hurry."

"Caitlyn?" the operator asked.

"Yes."

"I'll put you through."

"Caitlyn? What's wrong? Where's your mother?"

In an emergency, even detectives call for a mother.

"Detective Stanton, it's Nicola Cavan." I exhaled, bracing for the shit storm.

"My daughter is on the other line, Ms. Cavan. There's been an emergency. I'm going to hang up."

"I'm the emergency," I said. "I'm sorry."

"I see," he said. "That was a low blow, young lady. I thought you were better than that." He sounded more disappointed than pissed, which made things worse.

"I needed to talk to you now. It is an emergency. And I'm someone's daughter."

"How did you know I even had a daughter?" he asked, sounding fierce and pissed.

"You said on the radio."

"Right, well, that was my mistake," he said briskly. "This conversation is ending now. I feel badly for what has happened to you, but you don't get to make jokes involving my family."

"Wait, Stanton, please. I was just stalked by a man in a pickup. Don't hang up."

"Ms. Cavan, you should have called nine-one-one. I'm not your personal police officer."

"Please, just listen." I told him everything, from the red knit cap to the bumper stickers. BUILT FORD TOUGH. I must have said 429 a few times, because he said he'd gotten it, written it down, and I could stop.

"No letters from the rest of the plate?"

"No, sorry. I didn't catch all of it. He had a photo of me in his car, the newspaper clipping."

"I know. Ms. Cavan, you mentioned that. It's in my notes."

"There's something else. I think he left a bracelet, and it might be hers." I had been saving that, not wanting to sound too crazy too soon.

"A bracelet?" He hadn't expected that.

"A MedicAlert one. It says 'Allergic to bee stings,' and an ID number."

"Read me the number. I'll send an officer to come pick up the bracelet later," he said.

It's probably nothing, I could hear him thinking. But at least he was listening.

"You can call me Nico," I said. I was warming to him, now that he was taking me seriously.

"I'll stick with Ms. Cavan."

"Squamish Search and Rescue," I said again.

"I've written it down, thank you. Ms. Cavan?" I could tell by the way his voice curled into a fiddlehead that he was adding something he hadn't intended and would probably regret.

"Yes?"

"Are you sleeping at all?"

"Not much," I admitted.

"I think you should sleep more," he said. "You sound . . ."

"I know."

"We'll look into it," he said.

He hung up, either to get on the case, or before I could repeat the information again. I hoped he didn't think I was delusional. Then he wouldn't look into a damn thing.

I flipped open my laptop and sat cross-legged on my bedroom floor, wondering what search terms I could enter to help me find this man. I could try *Squamish Search and Rescue*, but anyone could buy a bumper sticker. Too much information had passed through the turnstile of my brain, and it stalled when I heard an email land, the sweet ping

237

like the triangle in band class. *Nico, how's things? Going indoor climbing tomorrow, you should try it. Walked past the Crocodile and thought of you. Listening to my first Modest Mouse album. When U coming back? Sean.*

I read it twice. It was friendly, for sure. *Thought of you.* I stretched out on my bedroom rug, willing myself to grow taller, wishing for a mother to explain everything to me.

They say you should appreciate the small things in life, which I used to think meant creatures like mice or lady-bugs, or trinkets like marbles or gumball-machine rings. Now I understand it's less literal and refers to the everyday or the simple. Verne had tried to be home more, to turn down overtime, even though it meant less money. I found I enjoyed it when we could make dinner together. I was thinking this while he gutted a red pepper, trying to scrape away the white seeds, which reminded me of baby teeth. I had told him about the man in the truck and shown him the bracelet before the officers came to collect it. We were both purposefully not talking about it while we waited to hear from the police.

"Do I ever get to meet that boy in Seattle?" he asked, keeping his head down so I couldn't see his face.

"What boy?"

"The one you met in Seattle who keeps emailing. Is he nice?"

"Yes, he's nice. How do you know he's emailing?"

"I have my ways. I'm a security expert," he said, mock

tough. I snorted, thinking about all the toga parties he'd broken up. There was lots of serious stuff, too, though—fistfights, thefts, and sexual assaults. "Actually, I just see you at your computer. Seriously, though, is he a good guy?"

"Seriously, yes. But I don't know if it's serious," I said, and laughed. My laugh sounded as if it came from some hidden vault deep in my body.

I woke to the squawk of the doorbell and shot up as if my body were an arrow fired into the hall. Verne was already there, dressed in track pants and a cotton shirt, still wearing his navy-blue slippers. I rushed to him, clamping my arms at my sides to keep my nightie from flapping.

"Mr. Cavan?" There were two Victoria Police officers, both in full uniform. I felt impressed for a second, at the badges and buttons, at this symbol of order in the world, before I allowed myself to realize what was happening. One officer was quite young, and the other was Stanton. I recognized him right away from my Internet searches. Detective Sergeant Stanton had silver hair and impressive high cheekbones. I'd imagined him to be in his fifties, but he looked younger, rangy. My legs wobbled. *Here it comes*, I thought.

"We've had a development on the case," said Stanton. He had the air of someone who could be called away at any time. He was important, unlike us. He got to the point. "Mr. Cavan, perhaps you'd like your daughter to wait in another room."

There was a pause. Our old heater groaned. I could vaguely hear the woman downstairs dragging a table, metal legs scraping on tile.

"No, no," said Verne. "It's her life. She should be here. Please come into the living room." We walked in silence and sat down. Both officers were tall and made the room seem tight, confined, and for a moment I couldn't breathe.

"Mr. Cavan, Ms. Cavan, we've had some information in the case of Annalee Jean Lester's disappearance on February 11, 1996. Following Ms. Cavan's encounter yesterday, we tracked down the owner of the 2002 gray pickup truck she sighted and made contact with the owner, Mr. Wayne Cruickshank. We also determined that the numbers on the MedicAlert bracelet corresponded to those designated for Annalee Jean Lester."

Verne nodded. I held my breath. Perhaps I would never breathe again. Did we have to say he should continue? I didn't know. I had lived all my life not knowing. Just say it, let it come. It could be no worse than all I had imagined so many nights, so many years.

"At first Mr. Cruickshank denied all knowledge of Ms. Cavan, but then he admitted having seen her on the street when he left the MedicAlert bracelet on the curb amid the refuse."

"I *knew* he left it," I said, my voice shaking. Stanton continued as if I hadn't spoken.

"During questioning, Mr. Cruickshank indicated he had heard the appeals for public participation in locating the whereabouts of Nicola Cavan and the media reports referencing the 1996 disappearance of her mother, Annalee Lester. He decided, at that point, that if Ms. Cavan was found safe, he would anonymously return the bracelet."

The man had made a bargain. If I had been found dead, too, it would have doubled his guilt. But he also wanted to get a look at me. Everyone did. Freako Nico. Annalee was no doubt the biggest thing that had ever happened to him. I could tell that with one glance into his truck.

"Mr. Cruickshank was in Garibaldi Provincial Park, close to Whistler, that February in 1996, where he was hunting, which is illegal in that park. He spotted a woman we now suspect to be Annalee Lester on the trail to Garibaldi Lake, where she was hiking. Believing her to be game, he fired a shot, which struck a female Caucasian, resulting in a fatal wound. We will need to consult with the coroner to verify these details," he said, regarding us with a rigid calm.

It was surreal to see those two officers sitting in the room where Obe and I played Risk, or used the Ouija board, or pawed through music magazines.

"Mr. Cruickshank stressed that he had not come to Victoria to harm Ms. Cavan, but rather to leave the bracelet for her to find."

"But then I saw him."

"Yes," said Stanton. He wasn't used to being interrupted.

"Where's the bracelet now?" I hadn't wanted to hand it over. It was bad enough that someone like Wayne Cruickshank had possessed the bracelet that my mother had worn on her slender wrist, the bracelet that was supposed to save her life.

"It has been admitted into evidence for the moment, but it will be returned. I understand that this news is shocking after all this time. Please be aware that we are following up on this lead with forensic reports and an exhaustive search of Garibaldi in collaboration with parks officials and local police. Mr. Cruickshank has expressed regret for his actions. Ultimately, he will answer to the courts, of course, and we must not do anything to jeopardize that process."

Stanton glanced at us both. I turned to Verne, whose face was bleached of expression.

"So she's dead," I said. "Are we supposed to feel glad that this man came forward, even though he shot her, shot her like a . . . ?"

I had been going to say dog, but people didn't shoot dogs, not usually. I sounded detached at first, like a student asking a question about an exam.

"What did he do with her, after?" I asked, my voice splitting open on the last word.

"Shhh, Nico, shhh," Verne said, circling his arm around me. "Enough for now, okay? Enough for now."

He looked at Detective Stanton and led me from the room. I bottled my sobs inside me until we got to the kitchen. I heard the front door close gently.

"See, Nico?" Verne said. "She never, ever, wanted to leave you." He took my hand and squeezed it tight, as if I were a little girl again, wearing pink mittens attached with a string.

CHAPTER 20

"JESUS DOESN'T WANT ME FOR A SUNBEAM"

It seemed cruel that my mother's love of wild places led her to be buried in an unmarked grave, far from anyone who loved her. There was no apology, per se, from Wayne Cruickshank, but there was an acknowledgment in the press: "It was an accident. I panicked." Some of the details made it into the newspaper. For example, Cruickshank buried her body in Garibaldi Park, but first he removed her MedicAlert bracelet. It was as if he wanted a memento, or perhaps to torture himself with the guilt. I couldn't understand most people, let alone a man who killed animals for fun.

The incident had not dimmed his taste for hunting, either. Cruickshank remained an active member of the Highway 99 Rod and Gun Club, a group that quickly put out a press release condemning his illegal and immoral behavior and banning him for life. *Hunters don't kill people; people kill people* seemed to be the reasoning. Cruickshank claimed he was debilitated by his own guilt, plagued by alternating bouts of nightmares or insomnia, and frequent panic attacks. When he saw my photo in the paper, he could no longer bear the guilt, or so he said, and decided to return the bracelet to me. Fortunately for us, he was stupid enough to get caught.

Perhaps my mother's own parents, my grandparents, feared she would die of a bee sting, especially since she so loved the outdoors. Yet she died in the dead of winter, hiking alone in the snow, surely not a bee in sight. What had she thought as she walked in the woods? She was probably looking forward to seeing Janey up in Whistler. Was she thinking about Nicola at home, waiting? Did she remember her promise to me and plan to keep it?

They were going to dig up her body. Verne didn't want me to know that, but I did. What choice did they have?

I couldn't sleep the night after hearing the truth, or the next. Something bad would happen to Wayne Cruickshank, the hunter, but it could never be enough. I hated him. He took my young, beautiful mother away, and then he panicked, and then he lied. Then he nursed the lie for years, putting me, and Verne, and Gillian, and Janey, and so many people through agony.

There would be a long list of charges against Cruickshank, including criminal negligence causing death and offering an indignity to a body. The rest didn't register with me after I heard that last one. Both my mother and Kurt

Cobain died from a gunshot, if he was really dead. I was getting confused about what I believed. I thought of Cobain's hunting cap, the one he wore ironically as part of his disguise, and got a chill.

After the news about my mother broke, Obe was constantly on me, phoning, emailing, and showing up at the door. He had put his new extracurricular activities on hold.

"So what are you going to do next, Nico? You have to think about tomorrow, too. Not just the past."

Since when did Obe talk like an *Oprah* guest? I could think of nothing to look forward to anymore. Even small things that I used to enjoy, like strawberry milk, made me sick. The world was completely drained of color, like *The Wizard of* Oz during the tornado scene. I was having pitchforks of stomach pain all the time, not just once in a while. I thought everyone else had been given some map, some diagram, to show them how to act.

"Verne is talking about buying a fixer-upper town house. He might have enough for a down payment. He thinks it would help to get out of this neighborhood."

"Get away from Mrs. Lemonpucker downstairs, too," said Obe, trying to make me laugh, so I snorted to please him.

"Sean, that guy I met in Seattle, keeps saying he's going to come visit. Not sure when. I told him there was news about my mother, but I don't want to explain it to him yet."

"Whooo," said Obe, or something to that effect. He seemed to want everyone to be coupled up now that he had that girl in Winnipeg, Kimber, who seemed remarkably average. Perhaps that was what he'd been waiting for: a kind, conventional girl.

"I do want to see where it happened," I said after a moment.

"Are you sure about that?" asked Obe. He'd gotten an ear pierced, and there was a halo of red inflammation at the site. I had been surprised, and wondered if the girlfriend approved. It was unlike Obe to put such effort into his appearance. Perhaps we were drifting apart. Things had been different since I returned. We weren't seven years old anymore, or even eleven, riding our crappy bikes around town.

"Yeah, I'm sure."

"Do you want to ask the Ouija, find out if you should?" he asked, holding a cup of tea I'd given him. He reminded me so much of a little old lady right then that I laughed.

"I think I don't want to know if it's a good idea. I just want to do it," I said. "Sometimes that's better. I was thinking of going at March break, but maybe I'll wait until the snow melts, I don't know. Everything seems to take a long time."

"Is Verne doing the night shift?"

"No, he's on days. He'll be home for dinner. He's trying not to work nights. The title of my memoir will be *Everyone's Worried About Nico*."

"Speaking of which, don't you have a history essay due tomorrow?"

"I'm finding it hard to concentrate, Obe. Or give a shit about school."

"I can stay until Verne gets here. Let's put on a disc and I'll study while you type."

Obe often did several things at once: eating, studying, listening to music, talking on the phone.

I would try. I would try to put it from my mind. My mother had been shot like an animal. She had been buried in the ground, left alone, while people walked above her, season after season. She would never come back. Annalee had broken her promise.

We went to my room, and I turned on my laptop. Obe sat on my bed reading a physics text while I typed. All the letters swarmed together on the screen like black ants. Maybe one day soon I would become the girl everyone had expected me to be: a girl who flunked out of school and got into trouble.

I made it to March break, despite my own predictions. I wasn't failing my classes, not yet, but I wasn't excelling. I was getting by. I carried the photo of my mother and Kurt Cobain at the concert in my wallet at all times as my protective talisman. I kept checking the Polaroid to make sure the image hadn't faded. Sean sent me regular emails, pretending to have seen Kurt Cobain around Seattle. *Saw Kurt today standing in front of Zig Zag Café. He was playing hacky sack*, that kind of thing. He meant it to be funny, like Elvis sightings, or *Where's Waldo?*, but it kind of stung. I couldn't tell him why, though. Obe would have understood, but Obe and I had known each other forever. Sean didn't know me well enough to ask me tough questions or have expectations, which made him my favorite person in the world at that time. He said he planned to see his brother during spring break, and sure enough, after a brief period of being grounded for staying out all night, he emailed to say he was on his way. *Coming 2 Victoria for 3 days to see my bro. R U in town? Let's meet up. Arriving Friday. . . .*

Spring had nosed its way into Victoria, gently. First the snowdrops with their fairy caps, then the purple and yellow crocuses. Then came the tiny forget-me-nots, as blue as Cobain's eyes. Many of the girls at school had already declared it tank-top weather, stripping down to the limits of the dress code.

At the sound of the last bell, the hallways flooded with kids trying to get out of there, off for family vacations, or babysitting jobs, or whatever. Obe, to his disappointment, was not going to Winnipeg due to a shortage of funds. Instead, he'd be stocking shelves at a shoe store, his new gig. His girlfriend, Kimmy or whatever, seemed to regard this change of plans as some kind of last straw and broke things off, deeming the entire affair a "winter fling." Verne was working most of the days, though he was home with a spring cold that afternoon. We'd made plans to see a few houses for sale. He'd been serious about that, and had already secured a real estate agent. Staring into the bowels of my locker, I grabbed a couple of empty Tupperware containers and my sketchbook.

I wouldn't miss the place. People had finally stopped talking about me. I was ignored again. I slammed my locker door shut and secured my headphones, drowning out all the chatter: the plans being made, the upcoming parties. The volume was cranked in case anyone should utter the phrase "Freako Nico."

I watched my own Converse slipping down the hall, tile by tile, while listening to the Pixies' "Where Is my Mind?" which was kind of my school theme song. I scampered down the front steps. It was warm and sunny, and the air outside smelled like soil the way spring does, a relief from the hallway stench of banana peels and sawdust.

Girls were screaming from the soccer field. Some kind of end-of-school game was going on, girls versus guys (or "chicks against dicks," depending on who described the event). It actually might have been a nice day to do something like that, though I had not been invited. I could see Liam already hotdogging, thumping the ball on his knee. I was not opposed to sports for others, but I was allergic to joining anything. Or at least, I told myself I was. A pair of satiny beige underwear had fallen out of a girl's bag, and Liam scooped it up off the grass and put it on his head, then bounced the ball again, grinning. I felt bad for the underwear, which made Liam look like a sad Kojak, that bald TV detective guy. At least Liam had finally found a use for his head.

Standing a few feet away from Liam was the thin, tall guy, the one who liked soccer. He had an English accent and he drew. Oh yeah, Bryan. I had forgotten the name of my own secret crush. He looked up at me just as Liam booted the ball. It bounced off his sternum, causing him to turn red.

I stopped to watch as the teams assembled, letting the Pixies' distortion fill my head. There were about thirty kids gathered. The girls' team had all put their hair in braids, as if they were part of some tribe. The ones with short hair wore paisley kerchiefs. For some reason the fact that they'd planned those details made my eyes sting. They belonged to something, even if it was just for a day. I had always made fun of teams and groups. The song ended and I took off my headphones to adjust them.

I heard a sound like a needle dragging across a record. It was a guy on a skateboard heading toward me, slicing down the sidewalk. I looked around. It was the same old Fernwood neighborhood: the brightly painted heritage houses, the old theater that used to be a church. I turned to look behind me, but no one was there. The guy was coming straight toward me.

There was a noise like *vup tup* as he flipped the board up and into his hand. He had on one of those puffy trucker hats that had been hip, then not, and then were hip again.

"Hey, Nico," said Sean, as if we'd just seen each other that morning. He looked older than I remembered, stronger. He was wearing a thin white T-shirt, army pants, a navy hoodie tied at his waist. "Your dad said you'd be here. My brother knew where the school was."

I couldn't talk for a minute. I could feel everyone watching me, waiting to see how this was going to play out.

"You called my dad?" I asked, remembering as I said it that Verne was at home, no doubt guzzling hot lemon drinks. He was a real baby about colds. I was aware of thirty pairs of eyes latching onto me. All the pregame posturing and preparation had slammed to a halt.

Sean turned to survey the field, suddenly aware of all the people, and then squinted at Liam with a puzzled look that morphed into disdain. If there had been a thought bubble over Sean, it would have read: *Dude. That is* pitiful. Liam flung the underwear back to the ground.

Sean shook his head as if making up his mind about something, and then leaned over and kissed me on the cheek. I forgot what I'd been about to say.

We must have started walking. My legs were moving. He reached for my hand.

"Do you want to get a coffee?" I asked, returning to my body again.

Over the following weeks, my social status at school had an uptick. It might have been due to the Sean sighting, or maybe I just stopped caring so much what people thought. In any case, it was better. Sean and I emailed, and he tried to get me to join this kind of friendship bulletin board on the Internet that American kids were into, and some kids here, too. I didn't need to fill my head with Nirvana so much, but sometimes I imagined what Cobain might say about certain things, like Myspace. ("No one owns space, Nico," or perhaps a less poetic "That's fucking fucked.")

I didn't need a website to advertise that I had, like, three friends. Verne and I had a nasty fight that ended up with him cutting off my Internet, because I kept searching Cobain, and Jasper Jameson, and music websites, and he said that was it until I started getting grades that reflected my "smarts." I had to check "the email" at the library, which I didn't really mind because the downtown library is a lively place, filled with people Gillian would call "marginalized." Obe went from just playing *Guitar Hero* to actually strumming a real guitar.

One afternoon in May the phone rang when I was home alone. I remember my nails were wet because I'd painted them (a rather sparkly shade of violet) in a fit of homework procrastination. When I picked up the receiver, there was silence, then someone playing the opening chords of "Redemption Song." I was confused, and then I realized who it was. Obe. I smiled into the phone until he stopped. Then he started laughing. "That's all I learned, Nico."

My grades got better and I made it to the summer. I babysat. I applied for a job at the grocery store and got it, and I'd often see the familiar elderlies from the neighborhood counting their quarters for premade sandwiches from the deli section. I went to Seattle to see Gillian again, this time with Verne, who met Sean briefly when we were walking past the Armory. Sean was working, so he couldn't talk long, but he and I had coffee later during his break while Verne and Gillian went back to the condo to start dinner.

We sat outside on a bench, and I could tell by the way

we sat apart, side by side, as if we were fishing companions on a dock, that we weren't going to be boyfriend/girlfriend. After a few minutes, he started telling me about this girl he'd started seeing who was seventeen and played bass. What I thought was: *Why do these chicks always play bass? Can't they be good at archery, or beekeeping, or something else?*

What I said was: "She sounds really cool." And I didn't feel like throwing myself from the top of the Space Needle. Maybe I had been through too much, or maybe Sean and I were meant to be friends.

"Can I walk you back to your aunt's?" he asked when his break was over.

"No thanks," I said. "Don't get in trouble with your boss. I think I know the lay of the land. Maybe I'll stop and have a snakebite at the Five Point," I said, to make him laugh.

And he waved as I walked away, which was nice, and when he couldn't see I started to cry, I guess because that hadn't worked out, and maybe the next thing wouldn't work out, and also because I was convinced that no guy would really like me, and also that my summer would be boring and sad. Still, it was nice to walk into Gillian's place and have Verne there, too. I tried to get him to ask her if she had a boyfriend, but he wouldn't. Gillian asked the questions, thank you very much. Verne slept on a cot in Gillian's living room, and I took the guest room again, and it felt cozy even though we were all in different rooms, and I think Gillian had finally forgiven me.

While listening to music on the ferry ride home, I

had another memory, one that had been lost in a crack. I thought I remembered lying in an orange tent filled with light, listening to my mother talking, and Verne, too, in low voices. I heard a hissing sound as they conversed, and then tin clattering, then soft laughter.

"Yes," said Verne, looking bewildered when I asked. "We went camping when you were three, at China Beach. You screamed blue murder when I showed you a fish I'd caught."

I closed my eyes and replayed the memory, the orange light, the laughter, while the Clipper pulled us home. I wondered if ferries brought me good luck after all.

Not long after that July trip, we held a memorial service for my mother at the top of Mount Doug, a viewpoint overlooking the city. Janey, Gillian, Obe, Grandma Irene, and I attended. We wanted to keep it private. It was a sunny, blustery day, and I imagined the wind scouring all the years of sadness from my skin. Janey and my dad embraced, maybe for the first time ever, and I had to look away, unable to bear witnessing how much they still missed her. I don't think it gets easier. I think survival is just habit: you survived one day, so surely you can survive another. Until you build your confidence up.

After the sentencing, the newspapers ran a photo of Wayne Cruickshank. I stared at the photos of his piggish eyes and his lopsided mustache. I was sorry that I couldn't forget his face. Some nights when my stomach ached, I'd lie awake thinking about my time with Cobain: the turtles in the bathroom, the smell of the woodstove, the sound of trees sweeping the windows, and the layers of quiet. I don't think I could find my way back to the cabin again, but I've never had a good sense of direction.

Obe passed his driver's test that summer, on his first try, and Nadia even let him borrow her little rusty VW Rabbit to drive around town. Obe's parallel parking was a thing to behold, precise and confident. It seemed strange to be driving around with him, just the two of us, and when I saw a couple of kids riding their bikes past the linen supply store, I did a double take, remembering us with our keys strung around our necks.

We drove to the breakwater, cranking Obe's new favorite album, *Reconstruction Site* by the Weakerthans, the band he'd discovered in Winnipeg.

"Do you miss Kimmy?" I asked Obe. I had been selfish, I realized, not asking him about the breakup.

"Her name is Kimber, actually. And honestly, not as much as I thought I would."

"You know, Obe, we can talk about you for a change. You don't have to worry about me anymore." I stared at his long fingers gripping the steering wheel at ten o'clock and two o'clock.

"I've been worrying about you a long time, Nico Cavan," he said, in his movie announcer voice. "And I intend to continue."

"I'm not sure I liked her anyway," I said, to be supportive. Even though I hadn't met her.

"Why didn't you like her, Nico?" he asked, but softly, so I pretended I didn't hear.

"I said, 'Why didn't you like her, Nico?'" he repeated. "I think you know."

Maybe I did know, but I couldn't say. I couldn't speak at all.

Obe and I both knew all the words to "The Reasons" by heart, so we yelled them out while he drove down Dallas Road by the sea.

"How I don't know how to sing. I can barely play this thing. But you never seem to mind, and you tell me to fuck off when I need somebody to. How you make me laugh so hard."

He parked the car, and I could see the happy dogs charging into the waves, which were churned up by the wind. How badly I still wanted a dog. I stopped singing for a minute, watching a man struggling to keep hold of an orange kite. What was a grown man doing flying a kite? Obe kept singing. He claimed he was a better singer since learning to play guitar, but I thought maybe he just sounded better to himself.

"I know you might roll your eyes at this, but I'm so glad that you exist," sang the Weakerthans and Obe.

The man lost control of the kite and it whipped away into the sky, slithering into the air like a salamander. I turned to Obe to see if he'd seen it, too, the kite's great escape, and that's when Obe kissed me. I was surprised, and he was surprised, but then we both smiled and looked out the window again. When he drove me home, a flare gun of panic went off in me, because it seemed something was about to change, but maybe that was good, or so I told myself.

Verne and I prepared to move into our new house, a tiny heritage bungalow with a moss-covered roof that needed fixing. "We'll get to it eventually," Verne had said, his new motto. A package arrived for me in early August. There was no return address. I was afraid to open it, even though I had given up on messages from the dead. I still had trouble being optimistic. It was a hardcover book, white with blue lettering on the cover: *Peroxide Blues* by Jasper Jameson. I turned immediately to the back to see the author photo, but in place of the headshot was the sketch I had done of Cobain, or Daniel O'Ryan, or Jasper Jameson—the man in the cabin. Next to the image was my name in small print: *N. Cavan*. The author bio was brief: *Jasper Jameson is a bestselling author. The Pacific Northwest is his home.*

I laughed, because I was delighted, and also pissed that he, of all people, had stolen my art. The sketch had been a gift, but it was meant for him. Something fluttered out of the book. It was a check made out to Nicola Cavan for ten thousand dollars. The signature at the bottom looked like a tangled hairball. On the memo part of the check he had scrawled: *For art school.*

Have you ever had a thought, and wondered if you would feel differently about it when you were older? Right then, I thought that someday, I would no longer believe that the man I met was Kurt Cobain. I knew that someday, when I was older, I would believe that the musician with the blazing blue eyes wanted to leave his drug-suffocated world so badly that he shot himself in a Seattle greenhouse on a rainy spring day. But today, I believe he's alive and driving a rusted Pontiac Phoenix, tending his turtles, and plotting his next story. And today is all I have.

I saw an interview online with Krist Novoselic that made me remember the owl items hidden under my bed, the ones I had saved for my mother. He said after Kurt Cobain died, he kept searching for left-handed guitars for him at pawnshops. Then he'd remember that Kurt was gone and he didn't need left-handed guitars anymore.

Kurt Cobain wrote a song about Frances Farmer, who was a glamorous film star who killed herself. You might think that she was the inspiration for Cobain naming his daughter Frances, but you'd be wrong. Frances Bean Cobain was named after a singer with the Vaselines, a Scottish indie band that Kurt Cobain revered to a feverish degree— which mystified some people. (They weren't *that* good.)

The song was called "Frances Farmer Will Have Her Revenge on Seattle," as if she were restless being dead and had left matters unfinished. The lyrics were about missing the comfort of sadness. And now I see what he meant. Sadness is comforting, in a way. It's a heavy wool blanket draped over your shoulders. No one will steal it from you. Happiness is terrifying. It's a small green shoot, as delicate as an eyelash or the small white cap of a snowdrop. It can be taken from you at any minute, any second.

After Kurt Cobain's body was found, his fans burned their plaid shirts. Grunge was dead. I know now that my mother is gone forever. What can I burn? Everything I have of hers is precious. While I grew up, she was out in the woods, buried under the snow in a forest by a lake like a fairy-tale princess. I'm still planning to visit there, the park, when I am ready. I want to see what she saw—the forest, the mountains, the lakes, and the sea.

There is a comfort in being sad. But I am ready to give it up.

ACKNOWLEDGMENTS

In 2012, I read a newspaper article mentioning a Nirvana concert in Victoria that took place in March of 1991. The show was at a forgettable nightclub and drew a small crowd. In just a few months, however, Nirvana would become the biggest band on the planet—rocketing to superstardom with the album *Nevermind*. That *Times-Colonist* article about the Victoria show got me thinking—which led to the idea for this story. Since then, I have read countless articles and many books about Nirvana and the life of Kurt Cobain, all of which served as background for writing this novel. I am particularly indebted to the works of Charles R. Cross: *Heavier than Heaven: A Biography of Kurt Cobain, Cobain Unseen,* and *Here We Are Now: The Lasting Impact of Kurt Cobain.* I also consulted *Kurt Cobain* by Christopher Sandford, *Grunge Is Dead* by Greg Prato,

Love & Death: The Murder of Kurt Cobain by Max Wallace
and Ian Halperin, as well as Kurt Cobain's own *Journals*.
I read dozens of online articles, blogs, websites, and zines.
And of course, I listened to Nirvana.

The major exhibition Nirvana: Bringing Punk to the
Masses at the fascinating Experience Music Project Museum in Seattle helped me actually see how much Nirvana
and Kurt Cobain meant to modern music. I would also like
to acknowledge the heartfelt interview given by Nirvana
bassist Krist Novoselic, taped as part of the EMP show, in
which he recalls searching for left-handed guitars for Kurt.
The story still brings tears to my eyes.

I acknowledge Winnipeg's the Weakerthans and their
songwriter John K. Samson for allowing me to reprint a
few lines of their wonderful, quirky song "The Reasons,"
from their unparalleled *Reconstruction Site* album.

Many thanks to the exceptional fiction teachers I've had
over the years, from Barbara Greenwood in elementary
school, to Jack Hodgins at the University of Victoria's writing program. More recently, Vancouver fictionista Zsuzsi
Gartner offered me the right manuscript consultation on
this novel at the right time, with her stellar advice, encouragement, and good humor.

My friend Shanna Baker tolerated my spontaneous out-
bursts of facts about Kurt Cobain's life and offered contin-
uous support. Kris Rice kindly provided insight into some
law-enforcement matters. And Adrienne Mercer Breen,
my close friend since the days Nirvana first ruled the air-

waves, read an early draft and offered insightful suggestions and kind words.

I am grateful to my warm and wise agent, Kerry Sparks, who saw something in this strange little story and thought that others would, too. You have truly changed my life. I am also indebted to my rock-star editor, Wendy Loggia, who made every page better with her astute comments and every day brighter with her cheer and encouragement. I am so fortunate to work with the whole Random House Children's Books team.

I'd like to thank my family, including my husband, David Leach, my son, A.J. (his first book is *Space Monkeys from Mars*), and my daughter, Briar. And appreciation in advance to Barrie and Marjorie Leach, who will no doubt lead promotion of the book in Ottawa.

My sister, Patricia, offered her unbridled support of this story, and all my stories. My father, Ron, who (perhaps sensing the futility) never suggested I do something "more practical" than writing. And thank you to my mother, Kathryn, who loved words, and books, and British Columbia's magnificent coast.

ABOUT THE AUTHOR

JENNY MANZER is a writer, an editor, and a former news reporter. She lives in Victoria, British Columbia, with her husband, son, and daughter. She loves music but never did see Nirvana play live.

Follow @JennyManzer on 🐦